"*I w...
and...*

"I'm not about to walk out on these kids the way I…"

The way I walked out on you.

Tony shoved back his chair and pushed to his feet. "Damn it, Becca, these kids need some consistency in their lives. They need someone who will commit their heart and soul to them. I can't let you get involved and then have you leave them if the going gets tough."

He started past her, moving toward the door. Rising, she put her hand on his arm to stop him.

A mistake. His skin was hot, the musculature under it rock hard. She yearned to move her hand along the length of his arm, from bicep to forearm to wrist, then lock her fingers in his.

His dark gaze burned into her, sending a honeyed warmth through her. Her heart thundered in her ears.

Then he covered her hand with his….

Dear Reader,

There's nothing more satisfying than baking something warm and yummy for your family. This fruit cobbler is exactly the sort of thing heroine Rebecca might make for the hero, Tony, as a quick and easy dessert. It really fits the bill as comfort food.

Regards,

Karen

Estelle's House Fruit Cobbler

Preheat oven to 375 degrees.

Filling:

6 cups berries or pared, cut-up fruit such as apples or peaches
3/4 cup sugar
1/3 cup flour

Combine berries or other fruit with sugar and flour; mix well and pour into 8x8 inch pan.

Note: If strawberries are used, add 1/4 cup tapioca

Topping:

1 cup flour
1 cup sugar
1 teaspoon baking powder
1/2 teaspoon salt
1 egg, beaten
1/2 cup butter (1 stick)

Combine flour, sugar, baking powder and salt and mix well. Add beaten egg to dry ingredients and stir until mixture is moistened but still crumbly. Spread topping evenly over berries/fruit in baking pan. Melt butter and drizzle over the topping. Bake 40 minutes or until topping is golden and fruit is bubbling.

THEIR SECOND-CHANCE CHILD

KAREN SANDLER

SPECIAL EDITION®

Published by Silhouette Books

America's Publisher of Contemporary Romance

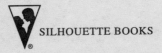

SILHOUETTE BOOKS

ISBN-13: 978-0-373-65437-6
ISBN-10:   0-373-65437-5

Recycling programs
for this product may
not exist in your area.

THEIR SECOND-CHANCE CHILD

Visit Silhouette Books at www.eHarlequin.com

Printed in U.S.A.

Books by Karen Sandler

Silhouette Special Edition

The Boss's Baby Bargain #1488
Counting on a Cowboy #1572
A Father's Sacrifice #1636
His Baby to Love #1686
The Three-Way Miracle #1733
Her Baby's Hero #1751
His Miracle Baby #1890
Her Miracle Man #1901
*Their Second-Chance Child #1955

*Fostering Family

KAREN SANDLER

first caught the writing bug at age nine when, as a horse-crazy fourth grader, she wrote a poem about a pony named Tony. Many years of hard work later, she sold her first book (and she got that pony—although her name is Belle). She enjoys writing novels, short stories and screenplays and has produced two short films. She lives in Northern California with her husband. You can reach Karen at karen@karensandler.net.

Chapter One

Tony Herrera studied his four-year-old daughter, Lea, across the kitchen table as she nibbled on her peanut butter and jelly sandwich without enthusiasm. She hadn't touched her cup of chicken noodle soup and had only taken a few sips of her milk.

In the six weeks since she'd been returned to him, she'd barely eaten enough to keep body and soul together. It broke Tony's heart.

"Do you want a cookie, *mija?*" Tony asked as he gathered up the lunch dishes.

Lea shrugged. Tony chose to take that as a yes. Setting the dishes on the tile counter in the big country kitchen, he lifted the lid on the cookie jar. As he flipped back the big-eyed cat head on the jar, an electronic voice sang out, *Three little kittens have lost their mittens...*

Lea's eyes brightened at the cheeky melody, her mouth curving into a faint smile. She took the chocolate chip cookie he offered her with a soft-spoken thank-you, then dipped it into her glass of milk.

Lea finding pleasure in anything, even a cookie, set off a mix of joy and pain inside him. He knew he had to be patient; as a former school psychologist, he understood better than most how long it might take Lea to recover from the trauma she'd endured. But it hurt so damn much seeing her suffer.

"Jana will be keeping an eye on you this afternoon," he reminded his daughter.

She nodded gravely. Lea liked Jana well enough. At twenty-three, his young assistant was barely older than the eighteen- and nineteen-year-old former foster children that his independent-living program served. But she kept an eagle eye on Lea when the little girl was in her charge.

While Tony and Lea ate their lunch, Jana had been conducting a preliminary interview with a potential new hire. After five previous candidates had proved to be a waste of his time, he'd gotten a clue and sent in Jana to vet the woman first. With her spiky blond hair striped with pink and myriad ear studs, Jana was far more representative of the independent program's students than Tony was. She'd never been a foster child herself, but she knew what it was like to turn eighteen with no skills and little education and have to find a way to support herself.

The applicant had to have the proper temperament to work with his initial group of six girls and two boys. The lives these former foster kids had led, their hard luck stories, had left many of them rough around the edges. There was no room in the program for someone who'd have a hissy fit over a few piercings or tattoos.

He picked up the woman's résumé from the kitchen table and scanned it again. Rebecca Tipton, from Los Angeles. A graduate of the California School of Culinary Arts' cordon bleu program. Pastry chef at some chichi four-star restaurant.

That had raised red flags when Tony had first read the woman's curriculum vitae. Why was she contemplating a move from sprawling Los Angeles to rural Northern California? Why abandon a high-profile position at a haute cuisine restaurant to teach former foster kids to bake apple pies at an isolated Sierra foothills ranch? What was Rebecca Tipton running away from?

Rebecca. Far too reminiscent of Becca, the name of his first love, his first wife. His initial irrational impulse when he'd read that name had been to eliminate the résumé from consideration. He'd had to force himself to replace it on the stack. Ridiculous to penalize a stranger for having the same first name as the woman who tore his heart out eleven years ago.

A knock on the kitchen door pulled him out of his brooding. Lea's wary gaze slid toward the door as she gripped her half-full glass of milk.

"It's just Jana, *mija*," Tony reassured her.

The solemn little girl watched as Tony crossed the kitchen and opened the door. Jana grinned up at him as she entered, but he saw the query in her brown eyes.

"Not too bad today," Tony told her softly. "She's a little quieter than usual."

"How's it going, sweetpea?" Jana said as she gave Lea a quick hug. Jana glanced over at Tony. "The lady's in your office."

"What do you think?"

"She's cool. Didn't so much as twitch at my hair or earrings. And Estelle likes her a lot."

As much as he valued Jana's opinion, Estelle Beckenstein's was the gold standard. His former foster mother had been a rock during his adolescence, a kind but firm disciplinarian who could sniff out a lie or a phony a mile away. If there was anything off-kilter about this applicant, Estelle would have sussed it out and sent her packing without wasting Tony's time with an interview.

He headed out the kitchen door, résumé in hand. As he strode toward his office—a converted barn that had once housed goats—the late July heat blasted him. It was bearable beneath the black oaks and ponderosa pines that dotted the side yard, but when he stepped into the sun's full glare, its intensity took his breath away.

When he first opened the door, the brilliance of the sunlight made it difficult to see in the relative dimness of his office. He could make out little more than the silhouette of a woman sitting with her back to him, her body more generous than Jana's tomboy physique, her hair shoulder length.

A chill trickled down his spine as he realized the woman bore a resemblance to his dead wife, Elena. In the shape of her body, the set of her shoulders, the length and color of her hair. He wondered if she would have the same chocolate-brown gaze.

Then, as his eyes adjusted to the light, she rose and turned toward him. The breath he'd regained in the coolness of his office vanished from his lungs as his gaze fell on that all-too familiar face.

It *was* Becca Stiles. The woman who had almost destroyed him.

* * *

Rebecca had anticipated a difficult reunion with Tony. She'd expected that storm cloud of anger in his face, the hardness in his usually soft brown eyes. As much as she wished otherwise, she'd come here knowing she might be escorted from the property the moment Tony realized that Rebecca Tipton was actually Becca Stiles.

But she hadn't been prepared for the heat that sizzled inside her, the throbbing low in her body. It had been more than eleven years since they'd last made love, since they'd been man and wife, but her body remembered his touch, his scent, every intimate word whispered in her ear.

His dark brown hair was shorter, but just as thick. His shoulders were broader, almost too wide for the Hawaiian shirt he wore, his arms more muscular. His hands were the same, blunt-fingered and strong, but like everything else about him, they spoke of power and competence. During their marriage, their lives had been filled with unknowns. Now it looked as if he'd found some answers.

As she gazed up at him, he leaned toward her, still angry but maybe pulled by the same memories. He almost reached for her; she could see his fingertips stretching toward her. Then he strode past her and put his desk between them.

"Sit," he said sharply, then bit out, "please."

Was he going to give her a hearing after all? Rebecca lowered herself back into the secondhand office chair.

"You remarried," he said.

"I hear you did as well."

Something dark flickered in his face. "I can't possibly offer you this position."

Rebecca dug in. "You know as well as I do that I'm perfect for the job."

"You're married. This is a live-in position, and I don't have accommodations for a couple."

"I'm divorced."

A long, silent beat as he took that in. Then his gaze narrowed on her. "Estelle didn't say a word when she recommended you."

"You wouldn't have even considered me if you knew. Even if no one else with my qualifications has applied."

"I may have named the program after Estelle, but she isn't the one that hires and fires here. I am." His gaze fixed on her, his dark eyes opaque.

She shivered, blaming the chill fingering down her spine on the gust of cool air spit out by the window air conditioner. Wrapping her arms around herself in self-defense, she considered the arguments she'd prepared, knowing in advance she'd have to fight for this job.

But did she really want to? Maybe he was right—she ought to return to her car. Head back down Highway 50, don those same imaginary blinders she'd worn on her way here as she passed the off-ramp to West Hills Cemetery. Take Interstate 5 south and drive back down to L.A.

Except what waited for her there was just more despair. In the two months since Rebecca's foster daughter, Vanessa, had been returned to her mother, Rebecca had been hollowed out with grief. One moment social services was dotting the i's and crossing the t's on Rebecca's adoption of Vanessa, the next they were calling to notify her that Vanessa's mother had regained custody. Now the five-year-old girl was lost to Rebecca forever. Just as her son was.

She had to at least plead her case with Tony. Hands linked in her lap, she tipped up her chin in challenge.

"You won't find anyone to match what I can offer. You

know from my résumé I have impeccable credentials as a baker. I've volunteered teaching cooking classes for two years at a local Boys and Girls Club. And you know as well as I do that my understanding of what these kids have been through in the foster system isn't just academic."

She'd spent a year in foster care when her parents were badly injured in a freak accident and required extensive rehab to get back on their feet. Estelle had lavished loving care on the frightened nine-year-old that Rebecca had been, becoming a second mother to her in that short time.

Tony's hands curled around the arms of his chair, the skin over his knuckles taut. "You'd be living here full-time. We'd be in each other's faces practically twenty-four/seven."

"It's been eleven years. We can put the past behind us."

"Some pasts shouldn't be forgotten."

That stung, although she probably deserved it. "I know I'd do a good job."

He almost seemed to consider it, then shook his head. "I have to think of the kids. They've all just been emancipated from foster care, and they're anxious enough about their futures. I can't increase their tension by adding you into the mix."

"Don't you think I deserve a chance?"

He shoved his chair back and pushed to his feet. "Damn it, Becca, these kids need some constancy in their lives. They need someone who will commit their heart and soul to them for the entire five months of the session. I can't let you get involved with them and then have you leave them in the lurch if the going gets tough."

He might as well have punched her in the gut. "I was nineteen years old, Tony. Young and confused. I'm not about to walk out on these kids the way I…"

The way I walked out on you. The silent words seemed to echo in the small space. On their heels came the harsher indictment—*The way I walked away from our lost son.*

He started past her, moving toward the door. Rising, she put her hand on his arm to stop him.

A mistake. Her palm fell on his biceps, just below where the wildly colored sleeve of his shirt ended. His skin was hot, the musculature under it rock hard. She yearned to move her hand along the length of his arm, from biceps to forearm to wrist, then lock her fingers in his.

His dark gaze burned into her, the visual connection sending a honeyed warmth through her. Her heart thundered in her ears, so loud she thought he must hear it, would know her self-control was slipping away.

Then he covered her hand with his. To break the contact, she thought, to get free of her. But his fingers lingered, his thumb stroking lightly across the back of her hand.

He pulled his hand back with a jolt, putting space between them at the same time. "You should go." His voice scraped across her nerves like rough silk.

She pulled in a long breath, willing her heart to steady. "I really want this job, Tony."

His gaze drilled into her. "Why?"

She barely understood the reasons herself. How could she communicate them to as hostile an audience as Tony?

She only knew that what once had seemed so important to her—working her way up the ranks in a four-star Los Angeles restaurant to become master patissier—now seemed like the most trivial of endeavors. Without Vanessa, Rebecca's home was filled with loneliness, a place to escape each day by going in to work at a job that no longer fulfilled her.

She tried to distill her turbulent thoughts down for Tony. "I want to feel as if I'm doing something important."

His jaw worked, tension in the motion. "So I should hire you so you can feel better about yourself?"

"You should hire me because I'm the best person for the job."

His expression grew cold. "The purpose of Estelle's House is to prepare those kids for life in the real world. You'll need to find another outlet to soothe your guilty conscience."

Even as she fought off the heavy weight of discouragement, she realized he was right. There were other opportunities out there she could follow up on, even some down in L.A. Why did it have to be here, with Tony? Because she wanted to be home again? Or because there were myriad unresolved issues between herself and her ex-husband?

He reached past her to open the door. Heat spilled inside, intruding on the coolness of the room. He waited, staring down at her.

She picked up her purse from beside the chair. "I've come all this way. Can I see the place before I go?" If she had more time with him, maybe she could persuade him to reconsider.

She could see he wanted to say no, but he gave her a brusque nod and gestured her outside. The afternoon sun had crept just past the towering pine tree beside Tony's office. The dappled light fell on a wrought-iron-and-wood park bench beneath the tree, giving an illusion of coolness. But in the growing warmth, even the short-sleeved knit dress she wore seemed stifling. This was brutal, San Fernando Valley–type heat, not the more temperate climate of West Los Angeles, where she rented her studio apartment.

Tony led her along a gravel pathway that wound between several structures. Overhanging oaks provided welcome shade. "This was once part of a two-thousand acre cattle ranch that's been subdivided over the years. Sam Harrison bought the eleven acres with the original ranch house and outbuildings as an investment. He leases the property to us for a modest fee."

"You're still in touch with Sam Harrison?" Another of Estelle's foster sons, Sam had hit it big as an author of edge-of-your-seat crime thrillers.

"Why wouldn't I be? Sam never left."

But she had. Rebecca didn't have to be a mind reader to divine that message. And although Tony had apparently found enough forgiveness in his heart for Sam's part in her departure, that absolution wouldn't extend to her. Yes, Tony's longtime friend had given her a ride to the airport, but then Sam had always been there to pick up the pieces.

They stopped at the building that faced the parking area, its construction much more recent than the decades old main house and what looked like a small cottage and bunk house beyond it. Fishing a key ring from his pocket, Tony pulled open the screen door and unlocked the back door. He paused to switch on the lights then stepped aside to give her room to enter.

Tony didn't know why the hell he was giving Becca—*Rebecca*—the grand tour. He wanted her out of here, the sooner the better. She looked too damned good, the thirty-year-old woman even more sensual, more intriguing, than the eighteen-year-old girl he'd married. She'd cut her long hair to just past her shoulders, lightening the dark color with caramel streaks, but her brown bedroom eyes were the same.

After that brief contact in his office, crazy thoughts had run rampant through his mind. Was her body as soft as it once was? Was her mouth as sweet, her sighs as tantalizing?

He had to focus not on the present, but on the past that still loomed large between them. He might have stuffed the worst of the memories into a remote closet in his mind, but if he let Rebecca get too close, he'd be trying out some of that old baggage pretty damn quick.

As she turned in a slow circle to view the brand-spanking-new bakeshop kitchen that Sam's donation had built, Rebecca smiled with delight. God, he'd forgotten the impact of her smile, sexy and beguiling all at once. There was a time she'd only needed to smile and he'd be all over her. Of course, as a healthy twenty-year-old, his hormones had generally trumped his good sense, sending him straight into her arms.

And straight into trouble.

Rebecca cast an appraising eye over the shiny stainless steel counters and eight-burner stovetop. She trailed fingers across the fronts of the two full-size ovens, resting her hand on the bowl of the forty-quart Hobart floor mixer. He remembered the feel of her hand on his arm, the warmth of it, the pressure. In those few moments in his office, he'd gotten hard, caught up in memories so swiftly.

He pushed aside the images as they threatened again to work their way into his mind. Arms crossed over his chest, he leaned against one of the stainless steel refrigerators.

She caught his gaze across the kitchen's central work island. "You did a great job putting this together."

He shrugged. "I hired a consultant."

"It's perfect." She smiled again, and his heart ached at the sight. "I have to admit I'm itching to toss some flour and yeast into that mixer bowl. Make some cinnamon rolls. Or apple turnovers. Or maybe a sweet braided loaf."

As she threw out suggestions, Tony could almost smell the yeasty scent of rising bread, taste the warm results fresh from the oven. Even before culinary school, she'd been an amazing cook. When they were married, when he'd come home from work tired and hungry, he always headed for the kitchen first. To breathe in the fragrance of her handiwork, then breathe her in, her own special scent.

He tamped down the persistent memories. This wasn't her kitchen. She wouldn't be cooking anything here.

Too edgy to remain with her in the cluttered confines of the kitchen, he strode through to the bakeshop's dining area beyond. Rebecca followed him, glancing back at the wide opening in the wall between the two rooms. He'd set up the cash register at one end of the pass-through for orders. They'd have a queue for takeout and another for dine-in, the fresh-baked treats conveyed to the waiting customers through the pass-through.

Large picture windows filled the side and front walls of the dining room, revealing beautiful views of the pine-and-oak-studded countryside. A potbellied stove in one corner would warm the space when the days grew cooler.

With a month to go until the Labor Day start of apple season, they hadn't yet set up the dining room. The eight-foot-long plastic folding tables were collapsed and leaning up against the wall beside stacks of chairs.

"How many can you seat?" Rebecca asked.

"A hundred, but we hope to do quite a bit of our business with takeout." To replace his thoughts of Rebecca's scent, the feel of her skin, he summoned up a picture of the dining room packed with people; long lines of customers eager to place their orders.

"How many students?" she asked.

With her question, he tumbled back into awareness of her. "We have space for eight. Two boys and six girls. Estelle's the official den mother. She stays with them in the bunkhouse."

"When do you start the program?"

"Life-skills classes have essentially started. Between Estelle and me, we're teaching them the basics of checking accounts, keeping up with monthly bills, the ins and outs of renting an apartment. Obviously learning how to run the bakeshop won't start until I hire a qualified instructor."

She faced him dead on. "Which I am."

"The program could crash and burn with the first session. Sam might get tired of funding a losing proposition. You could be out of a job in five months."

If he'd hoped to discourage her, he could see from the bright interest in her eyes that he'd failed. "Do you have a menu yet?"

In spite of himself, her persistence lit a spark of empathy in him. "It'll depend on what fresh produce is available in the area."

"I love cooking with fresh, local produce." She glanced over at him, and he could see the final silent plea in her eyes—*Give me a chance, Tony.*

But he damn well wasn't stumbling into that trap. "I'll walk you to your car so you can get on the road." The quicker he could get her out of here, the better.

But she didn't budge. "It's seven hours back to L.A. I didn't plan to do the round-trip in one day."

"You're not staying here."

"Of course not." Her soft brown eyes, filled with secrets he told himself he didn't want to know, fixed on him. "I made a reservation in a motel in Placerville."

The El Dorado County seat was five miles down the hill. "Then you'll want to go check in."

"I thought I'd stay a couple nights. Spend some time visiting with Estelle."

She almost seemed to be daring him to object. But he couldn't deny her the time with Estelle. Although Rebecca had lived with Tony's foster mother only a year, Estelle had remained an important constant in Rebecca's life. He'd just have to lock himself up in his office while she was here.

She wandered over to the front window and walked along it. She seemed to be admiring the vibrant pansies and petunias the girls had planted in a flowerbox on the other side of the glass. But she looked so lost, as if he'd dealt her a fresh blow.

Damned if he'd let himself feel bad. Rebecca was no longer his responsibility.

"Did you stop at the cemetery on your way here?" he asked.

She glanced at him, then back out the window. "No."

Was that guilt he saw in her eyes? Did she think he would deny her a visit to West Hills while she was here? "I'm sure Estelle would go with you. It's been a few months since she was out there last."

Her face blanched, and her hand shook as she pressed it against the window glass. "Where's Estelle now?"

A long-dead urge—to take care of her, see after her well-being—rose in him. He ruthlessly thrust the impulse aside. "She's in the bunkhouse with the kids. I'll take you over there."

"Thanks." She turned toward him, her composure regained.

They retraced their steps through the kitchen and back out into the summer heat. The bunkhouse was beyond the main house and his office, just past the small two bedroom cottage where Jana lived. The resident cooking instructor would live there as well, when he hired her. Although neither of the two résumés remaining were particularly promising.

As they passed the cottage, he stopped in its shade. "Rebecca."

She looked up at him, her expression composed, but he sensed turbulence under the surface. "Yes?"

He shouldn't even ask, should just keep on walking. Take her to Estelle and return to his office. Call the numbers on the last two résumés.

"Why does it matter so much? You have a life in L.A., a good job there."

Her gaze slid from his. "I needed to come back home."

"Then find a job at some fancy restaurant down in Sacramento." Anywhere away from here.

"I want work that means something." Tears glittered in her eyes. "A way to fill…"

He waited for her to finish, but she stepped away from him, her face averted. He'd never liked seeing Becca cry. That day in the hospital when he'd felt so frozen with grief, her loud, ugly sobs had shredded his heart.

They continued toward the bunkhouse, leaving the words unsaid. Her palpable sadness unsettled him, both because he didn't want to see her hurting and because he didn't want to care.

When they entered the converted bunkhouse, the noise level was deafening, the six girls and two boys making exuberant conversation in the living room. Draped over secondhand sofas and easy chairs, they filled the space with loud, youthful energy.

Estelle sat squeezed on one sofa between Brittany and Ari, who were flanked by Ruby and Colleen. The boys, Kevin and James, filled the other sofa with their lanky bodies. Serena and Katy perched on the sofa back. Jana had come over with Lea, who leaned against Estelle, her somber brown eyes taking in the raucous gathering.

"Lea, your daddy's here," Brittany called out.

Lea's head swung around as he stepped into the living room. She smiled up at him. Then her gaze moved past him to Rebecca. The little girl's face lit as if a flame had burst within her. She mouthed the word *Mama*.

Then as fast as her small legs could carry her, she ran across the room and launched herself into Rebecca's arms.

Chapter Two

Tony had a daughter.

As Rebecca held the sweet weight in her arms, breathing in her little-girl smell, she felt as if her heart had just been carved from her chest. Lea might be a year or so younger than five-year-old Vanessa, her hair might be dark and long where Vanessa's was sandy blond and cut in a short cap, but she felt the same in Rebecca's arms.

Estelle had only told Rebecca that Tony had married, that he was now divorced and had been for a few years. She'd never mentioned a little girl. Maybe because Rebecca had just sobbed out her grief over the phone about the adoption falling through, that Vanessa would be returning to her mother. Estelle might not have wanted to rub salt in that wound by mentioning Tony's perfect little girl.

Tony reached for Lea, tried to pull her small hands

from around Rebecca's neck. "Come on, *mija*. Let's go back to the house."

Lea just clung more tightly, burrowing deeper under Rebecca's chin. "It's okay," Rebecca said. "I can hold her a while longer."

She wanted to hold her forever. Close her eyes and pretend that the tragedy of twelve years ago had never happened, that this little girl was the baby she'd carried in her womb back then. Despite the illogic of the difference in gender and age—Alejandro had been a boy and would be twelve years old now—she wanted desperately to believe the fantasy.

The taller boy whacked the other on the shoulder, gesturing for him to get up. "Come sit down," the dark-haired boy said as he and his compatriot cleared the sofa. The Hispanic girl and the blonde who'd been sitting on the sofa back slid down onto the cushions on the far end.

Rebecca sat at the opposite end, facing Estelle and the other girls. She settled Lea in her lap and smiled across the room at Estelle. She was surprised by how much the older woman had aged since Rebecca had seen her last—seven years ago when she and her late husband, Jake, had visited L.A. Her dark hair showed more salt than pepper, and the lines on her face cut deeper than Rebecca would have expected in a woman only in her mid-sixties.

Lea wriggled in Rebecca's arms, distracting her from her observation of Estelle. Then, with a sigh, the little girl relaxed against her.

Estelle and Tony exchanged a meaningful look, and Rebecca could see the query in the former foster mother's eyes. Tony shrugged in answer. The kids all stared at her in avid curiosity.

"This is Rebecca Tipton," Tony finally announced. "She's…an old friend."

He reeled off the names of the six girls and two boys, a rainbow of ethnicities, each bearing numerous piercings and at least one tattoo. Hairstyles ranged from Ruby's relatively sedate close-cropped Afro to James's blond Mohawk. Their attitudes ran the gamut as well, from blond Katy's tentative friendliness to dark-haired Serena's barely veiled mistrust.

But their loving deference for Estelle was crystal clear. They called her Grams. Their gazes would zoom in on her as they spoke, as if they sought validation, reassurance, with each word. The girls, sitting on either side of her, had their arms draped around Estelle's shoulders. The others all but turned themselves inside out looking for ways to please her.

"Can I get you soda, Grams?" Kevin asked, snake tattoo flexing as he waved an arm toward the kitchen.

"There's some of the cookies we made, Grams." Brittany's lip ring bobbed as she spoke. "You want some?"

Ari fixed Rebecca with her exotic dark gaze. "Was she a foster with you, Grams?"

Estelle gave Rebecca a fond smile. "Only for a year. Her parents were friends of mine."

"Were they druggies?" Serena asked baldly. Rebecca suspected the Hispanic girl had firsthand knowledge of drug-addicted parents.

Rebecca shook her head. "There was an accident. They were so badly hurt they couldn't take care of me."

"Rebecca had no other family. Like you, Ruby." Estelle patted the girl's knee. "So I took her in until her folks could get back on their feet."

"Did she meet Tony at your house, Grams?" Serena demanded.

"That's right," Rebecca told her. "And we kept in touch over the years." She omitted the part of "keeping in touch" that involved her unplanned pregnancy and their brief marriage.

Standing beside the sofa, Tony loomed over her, his expression unwelcoming. Then she could see it change, soften, as he gazed down at his daughter.

"She's asleep," he said quietly, exchanging another significant glance with Estelle. "Jana, would you put her down on one of the girls' beds and stay with her? Rebecca and I have to talk."

Rebecca immediately missed the little girl's warmth when Jana lifted Lea from her lap. Tony offered his hand to her, but Rebecca hesitated, reluctant to risk the contact. But it would be rude to refuse his help, not an example she wanted to set with the kids. She might only be here a day or two visiting Estelle, but she could model polite behavior in that time.

Although he let go of her hand after she gained her feet, she felt the pressure of his touch on the small of her back as they started toward the door. Just as palpable were the gazes of Estelle and the eight foster kids, watching as they departed.

Tony kept his hand on her as they walked along the path. "Let's get in out of this heat."

He guided her toward the main house, the dampness where his hand rested bringing back memories of lovemaking on hot summer nights. They'd lie under the ceiling fan in their tiny apartment, both of them slick with sweat, creating a heat that rivaled the season's.

Maybe the same thoughts had occurred to him, because

he dropped his hand finally as they reached the big white farmhouse. They climbed the wide steps and crossed the broad front porch together. Then she waited as he opened the screen door and front door.

Her breath caught in her throat as she looked around her at the homey living room. She'd lived with her parents in a ranch-style down in the Sacramento Valley, not a two-story like this one. Her home was situated in a crowded Rancho Cordova cul-de-sac rather than on eleven acres in the Sierra foothills as Tony's was. But everything about this place shouted home—from the rumpled afghan on the sofa, to the kitschy knickknacks displayed on end tables and shelves, to the nicked coffee table cluttered with children's books.

If she could have dreamed of the perfect home for herself, this rambling farmhouse would have more than fit the bill. During lonely nights in her West L.A. studio apartment, the four close walls reminding her of the emptiness of her life, she imagined more than once she might someday have a home like this. Standing in Tony's living room, she wanted nothing more than to settle in the well-worn recliner, cuddle up with one of the cross-stitched pillows and sleep away the pain lodged in her chest.

But this wasn't her house, and she had no right to dream. She avoided the recliner, sitting instead on the sofa and locking her hands together in her lap. "Can you explain to me what just happened with Lea?"

On his feet, Tony paced, fingers raking through his hair. "I don't know. Or maybe I do. But I don't want to…" He speared Rebecca with his dark gaze. "I just know I have to get you out of here before she wakes up."

The vehemence of his words struck her like a blow. "I don't understand."

He pressed his lips together as if to tamp down his emotions. "Lea is four years old, but she's only been living with me for about six weeks."

"She's adopted?" A sense of injustice swamped her that Tony could achieve that miracle and she could not.

"She's mine. Mine and Elena's. Lea was two when Elena and I divorced."

"Did your wife get custody? Is that why Lea didn't live with you?"

"I had full custody." Bitterness edged his tone. "My ex-wife stole her from me."

The shock of that revelation rolled over Rebecca. "She's had her all this time?"

Tony strode back across the room with restless energy. "It took me two years to find her. First I tried on my own. Then I hired a crooked P.I. who took my money but couldn't find an elephant in his own backyard. Fortunately I made contact with Darius Jones again."

She remembered Darius, intense and dark-haired, from Estelle's. "He found Lea?"

"Within two months. He's a private investigator now. Specializes in skip-trace and missing people. He located Lea in foster care in Reno. It took DNA testing to prove she was mine."

"How did she end up in foster care?"

Tony stilled, his eyes squeezing shut for a moment. "Elena had been using an assumed name for her and Lea. Got some counterfeit documents somewhere."

He released a long sigh. "From what Darius and I were able to piece together speaking with the foster mother and Elena's coworkers, Elena did the best she could for Lea. Arranged for babysitters, sometimes a different one every week, but at least Lea had some kind of care. But then…"

His voice trailed off, and she could see the grief in his face. "One night Elena died in her sleep of a brain aneurism. Lea sat by her side for hours waiting for her mother to wake up before a coworker came to check on her."

"Oh, no." She felt sick at the thought of that sweet little girl sitting vigil by her mother's body.

He settled on the arm of the sofa opposite her. "In the six weeks since I've had her back, she scarcely says a word. Between fear and nightmares, she hardly sleeps. She tolerates my hugs, will stay with Jana or Estelle willingly enough, but has to be persuaded to hold their hand. She's never thrown herself into their arms."

"So what she did with me…"

"Is completely out of character for Lea. At least the Lea I've come to know in the last month and a half. The little girl she was two years ago, before Elena took her…happy, open, loving…" He hunched on the sofa arm. "That little girl is gone. Or has been until today."

"But I'm a complete stranger to her. Why did she respond that way to me?"

"I have a guess. Let me show you something." He hurried to the stairs, then took them two at a time to the second floor. When he returned, he brought back what looked like an acrylic photo box. "This is from three years ago."

He held the picture out to Rebecca. As she studied it, Rebecca could see the cursory resemblance to herself. Both of them with their dark hair in a shoulder-length cut, both with chocolate-brown eyes. Rebecca didn't have the luscious caramel skin or high cheekbones that bespoke Elena's Latina heritage. Rebecca's face was much plainer, the consequence of her family's Heinz 57 mix.

"Back when I first met Elena…" Tony glanced away as color rose in his face. "Estelle noticed a slight resemblance between you and her. I wasn't so willing to see it. But when I saw you today…" His gaze travelled her body from head to toe. "You've changed. The similarity is stronger."

Shivering under his regard, Rebecca handed the photo back to Tony. "She can't think I'm her mother come back to her."

"I doubt it. But she wants her mother so much she's willing to let herself believe you might be her." He scrubbed at his face. "You understand why you have to leave. If she sees you again, if that attachment grows even deeper…"

"What about Estelle? I'd still like some time to visit with her."

"She can meet you in town while you're here. She's not driving anymore, but Jana or I can bring her. I'm sure Estelle would appreciate going with you to West Hills."

Rebecca's stomach tightened with guilt and shame. After almost daily visits that first year, more than a decade had passed since she'd been there. But it all fit together, the reason she left Tony, the unbearable horror of her loss making it impossible to visit that grave with its small black headstone.

Maybe with Estelle at her side, she could do it. Bear the pain of again seeing that name carved in granite.

Or she could simply leave. Drive a few hours, then hole up in a hotel somewhere. Forget about Estelle. Close the door once and for all on her life with Tony, on their dead son. Pretend she'd never met James and Colleen and Ruby, forget the way they'd already begun to snag her heart during those few minutes spent with them.

Ignore the fact that even within that brief time, she knew them as well as she knew herself. It hurt to think of driving away from here today, never seeing them again.

Rebecca got to her feet, reaching for her handbag with an automatic gesture. "My purse is in the bunkhouse."

"I'll get it." He started for the door. "I'll meet you by your car."

After he left, Rebecca took a last look around her at the lived-in untidiness of Tony's home. Giving herself a moment to pretend, she folded the afghan and laid it neatly over the back of the sofa. She gathered up the books, stacking them in order of size, from biggest to smallest, and set them in the center of the coffee table. If she'd had the time, she would have dusted the shelves of ceramic knickknacks and the unbreakable bric-a-brac on the end tables, then corralled the dust bunnies from the drapes with a vacuum.

Instead, she pointed her feet out the door. She'd parked her Corolla two-door under the shade of a pine tree two hours ago. The sun's progression in the sky had shifted the shade and left the Toyota baking in the heat.

Sitting on the hood of the car in the scrap of remaining shade, she watched for Tony's return. She tried to suppress the despair that welled up in her, a familiar companion. She'd wanted this job so much. Even having to deal with Tony again, resurrecting the old conflicts between them, hadn't diminished her desire to work here, live here, to help these kids.

Tony finally emerged from the bunkhouse, Rebecca's purse tucked under one arm. He strode quickly toward her, glancing back over his shoulder.

When he reached Rebecca, he shoved the purse into her hands. "She's awake. Jana and Estelle are trying to keep her distracted."

Rebecca dug for her keys. Her hands shook, and she had trouble stabbing the key into the lock.

She'd just gotten the door open when a shriek from the direction of the bunkhouse grabbed her attention. There was Lea, starting toward her, Jana in pursuit. Jana caught the little girl and as she wrestled to hold her back, Lea screamed again. Even from thirty yards away, Rebecca could see her terror.

Tony stepped between them, no doubt hoping to hide Rebecca from his daughter's view. But the little girl wasn't fooled.

"Don't go!" Lea shrieked. "Come back!"

Rebecca looked up at Tony, saw the agony in his dark eyes. Then he took Rebecca's keys and purse from her and moved aside. He nudged her in Lea's direction.

Rebecca didn't need any more encouragement. She hurried toward Tony's daughter just as Jana let her go. Moments later, she was holding the little girl tight, Lea's heart beating frantically against her own.

Exhausted by lack of sleep and the emotions of the afternoon, Lea had crashed again, this time on the living room sofa. Rebecca had had to assure his daughter again and again that she wouldn't be leaving, that she would be there when Lea woke up. All Lea had to do was call Rebecca's name and she'd be there as quick as her feet would carry her.

Now Rebecca sat at the kitchen table with a glass of iced tea in front of her. Tony had served himself a glass as well, but his throat felt as if a powerful hand clutched it, and he didn't see how he could swallow so much as a sip of tea.

He leaned against the breakfast bar, the sweaty tumbler chilling his palm, the ice cubes rattling as his hand still trembled. Rebecca ran a finger down her glass, her gaze following the drops of moisture as they trickled down.

Forcing his throat to relax, Tony took a drink. Now that they finally had a chance to talk, he had to make sure they were on the same page. "This changes everything."

She glanced up at him warily. "What do you want to do?"

"What I want…" He set his glass down on the tile counter. "I want you out of here. But that's not going to happen. Lea is more important than my petty concerns."

She dipped her head in acknowledgment. "I'll stay as long as she needs me."

He pushed off from the counter. "You've got the job. I'll need at least a commitment for the entire five-month session for the kids' sakes. Can you promise to stay that long?"

She looked offended. "Of course. Longer if you need me."

"Let's get something straight, Rebecca." Planting his hands on the table, he leaned toward her. "*I* don't need you. The kids do and Lea does. Whatever we had…" Bile burned in the pit of his stomach. "It's gone. Destroyed."

She'd made damn sure of that when she'd left. The physical attraction he still felt toward her, that was nothing. A trivial insignificance he would just ignore.

Even with him inches from her, there was not a trace of intimidation in her eyes. "I didn't come here looking to renew old times. I just want to help these kids. And now your daughter."

"I'll still be looking for your replacement for subsequent sessions. And Lea's working with a counselor. She'll be able to ease my daughter into accepting your eventual departure."

She tipped up her chin. "Understood."

He'd made his point; her response told him his message had hit home. He should back off, get another drink of tea. Or better yet, dump it on his overheated head.

What he shouldn't be doing is stare at her mouth, moist from the tea, or contemplate the dainty onyx earrings she wore and how it would feel if he stroked her lobe with his fingertips. He most certainly shouldn't let himself think about how warm her skin was under the flowing skirt of her dress, or how the narrowness of her waist would feel contrasted with the generosity of her hips.

He shoved back from the table, moving to the other side of the breakfast bar. "I've got some work to do in my office. Would you sit with Lea, then bring her when she wakes?"

She nodded, lips parted, eyes wide. If she saw something of his fantasies in his face, he didn't want to know it.

"When will you tell the kids?" she asked.

"When Lea wakes up. We'll go down to the bunkhouse, let the kids know you've been hired as their cooking instructor."

He backed out of the kitchen, nearly running down the side steps and across the yard. What he really needed was a cold shower, not this jog in the searing afternoon sun. But there was no way he was returning to the house with Rebecca there.

Back in the coolness of his office, he slumped in his

chair. He could survive Rebecca's presence. If it meant a start to the healing process for his daughter, he could survive anything. Just because his body was reverting to adolescent lust didn't mean he had to pay any attention to its urgings.

His gaze fell on the bottom drawer of the rusty, second-hand file cabinet beside his desk. He knew what he'd stuffed away behind the hanging folders in that drawer. Knew he should have thrown it away a decade ago. It had certainly caused him more pain than happiness looking at it over the years.

Maybe he ought to pull it out now, carry it to the Dumpster out behind the bakeshop. Take another step in obliterating that part of his life.

He slid open the drawer all the way, pulled the fat hanging folders toward the front. Felt for the framed photograph sitting face down in the back. Sank down into the chair with the picture in his hands.

And stared at Rebecca's smiling face—Becca then—and his own youthful grin. It hadn't been much of a wedding, just a quick trip to the justice of the peace and a party at Estelle's afterward. She'd bought a pretty knee-length cocktail dress at a thrift store, choosing a size larger so it would fit around her expanding middle. He'd borrowed a dress shirt and jacket from Estelle's husband, Jake. He and Becca had been far happier that day than they'd had any reason to be.

The framed photo digging into his hand, the past stabbing his heart, he thought about the Dumpster. He knew it was the right place for this last memory of his and Rebecca's short marriage.

But he put the picture back in the drawer and kicked it shut.

Chapter Three

Lea didn't wake until after six that evening. Rebecca, curled up in the recliner, had dozed herself, rousing when Lea's small hand patted her knee. The worried crease in Lea's brow set off a pang inside Rebecca. She could imagine the little girl thinking of her mother, wondering if Rebecca would wake up as her mother hadn't.

Rebecca found a note propped up on the stack of books on the coffee table. *We're all in the bakeshop.* Tony's hasty scrawl hadn't changed. His mind always moved so fast, his fingers would struggle to keep up when he wrote. He was scribbling shorthand in his notes long before the Internet, LU4EVR a favorite sign-off.

Except forever hadn't lasted nearly as long as they'd thought it would. Even as she told herself the stillbirth hadn't been her fault, she couldn't shake the feeling that if she'd been stronger, she could have somehow better nurtured her baby. Then maybe they could have kept a grip on their marriage. But she'd let go of both, the first loss completely out of her control, the second due to her weakness.

As Rebecca stared down at the note, Lea pulled at her skirt. "Becca." She spoke so softly, Rebecca had to strain to hear. "Where's Daddy?"

"We'll go find him. But first let's go wash our hands and faces."

Lea pointed the way to a downstairs bathroom where she carefully watched Rebecca splash water on her face, then mimicked her actions. After they'd cleaned up, Rebecca found a comb and tidied Lea's long dark hair. All the while, the little girl always had one eye on her as if to be sure Rebecca wouldn't vanish when she wasn't looking.

Rebecca neatened her own hair, choosing to ignore the wrinkles she'd put in her dress during her nap. "Do you want to change, sweetheart?"

Lea's hot-pink shorts and T-shirt were both smudged with grape jelly. She shook her head, taking Rebecca's hand and towing her from the bathroom.

Outside, the heat had mellowed a bit, the shadows of the pines stretching across the lawn, pointing east. As they approached the back entrance of the bakeshop, Kevin came out with two empty restaurant-sized cans. He quickly tossed them in the Dumpster, then hurried back to get the door for Rebecca.

"Brace yourself," Kevin said with a cheeky grin. "It's crazy in there."

Kevin's warning turned out to be an understatement. Four of the girls were at the stove arguing about what else should go in the sauce, James was flirting with Ari and

Katy, and Jana was balancing herself on a chair from the dining room, trying to retrieve a stack of dishes from a high shelf. Estelle sat out of the way on a kitchen stool and Tony was MIA.

Grabbing Jana's arm to haul her from the chair, Rebecca put two fingers in her mouth and let out a shrieking whistle. The room grew suddenly quiet. With a roll of paper towels in his hand, Tony poked his head out of what Rebecca guessed was the dry stores.

"Ruby, turn down the gas on that sauce or you'll burn it. Serena, put a lid on the pasta water or it will never boil. If you haven't added salt, put that in first. Colleen, use a cutting board to chop that onion. That stainless steel countertop will ruin the knife. Brittany, you come help me find makings for the salad."

She turned her attention to Jana, the boys and the two remaining girls. "The rest of you, go get the tables set up in the dining room. Estelle, can you supervise them and take Lea with you?"

The little girl kept her fingers tightly meshed with Rebecca's. "Want to stay with you."

Rebecca bent and kissed Lea's cheek. "I could really use your help out there. Keep the big kids organized. Can you do that?"

Lea pressed her lips together in consideration, in that moment the spitting image of her father. Rebecca wanted to take her in her arms and smother her with kisses. Instead she straightened and nudged Lea toward the dining room. Her feet dragged at first as she walked beside Estelle, then when one of the girls called her, she ran the rest of the way.

Tony handed the paper towels to Brittany. "Put those

up." He took Rebecca's arm and pulled her out of earshot. "I don't like you coming in here and ordering them around. I haven't even told them yet."

Rebecca shook off his grasp. "So I should have let Ruby burn dinner? Let Colleen dull the edge on an expensive knife? Look the other way when Jana's choice of stepladder would give a California OSHA inspector fits?"

"No." Realizing several sets of eyes were directed their way, Tony angled his back toward them. His chest rose and fell as he took in a breath. "You did the right thing. You just caught me off guard."

She felt the same way just standing near him. If not for their avid audience, Rebecca wasn't sure she'd be able to keep from brushing his arm, leaning in close to him to feel the heat radiating from his body.

She edged away. "Maybe you should tell them now."

"Right. Sure." He lingered a moment, staring down at her, then turned abruptly away. In the doorway to the dining room, he called everyone over. "You might have figured out that Rebecca knows a little bit about running a kitchen. I've hired her as your cooking instructor. She'll be staying with us for at least the duration of the first five-month session."

Most of the kids seemed happy with the announcement. Katy's unbridled exuberance was tempered by Ruby's reserve and Serena's scowl, but Rebecca wasn't about to force them to like her. Being likeable wasn't part of her job description. She'd just take a page out of Estelle's book and give them respect and unconditional love.

While she sent Brittany to the walk-in refrigerator for bagged lettuce, Rebecca searched the dry stores for a box of hairnets Tony had told her he'd bought. Tony, using a sturdy stepladder instead of a plastic chair, handed down to Jana the stack of plates and bowls she'd been after. Rebecca dispensed the hairnets to her reluctant crew, informing them that they were to be worn every time they worked with food, no exceptions.

They filled two tables set end to end, serving themselves from a generous bowl of pasta and the massive pot of sauce. Rebecca insisted everyone take a serving of salad, squeezing in a short lecture on balanced diets when they complained. Tony's group was in turns surly and rude, awkward and insecure, but Rebecca could see the kids had big hearts. They truly wanted to learn. They knew that as much as they wanted to be independent, they needed help to get there.

It might not be a conventional family, but it was a family nonetheless. This kind of noisy gathering was everything she'd longed for as a child. Her heart filled with gratitude at the opportunity to be here with the kids, with Estelle, with Lea.

With Tony. Despite the peril in feeling anything but neutrality toward him, the new community she'd entered had upended her emotions. Added to that, the partial responsibility she'd been given for Lea's well-being made it difficult to keep her heart from straying into dangerous territory. The past they'd shared was gone, buried with the baby they'd lost. But a part of her had never given up on that dream.

She had to surrender it here and now. She'd only hurt herself wishing for a revival of those what-ifs and might-have-beens.

Kevin pulled her out of her reverie. "Can I get you more salad?"

"Sure. Thanks." She handed him her bowl.

Unbidden, her gaze slipped along the table to Tony sitting at its head. His eyes were fixed on her, mysteries and secrets in their dark brown depths. It seemed as if a string stretched between him and her, taut and vibrating with awareness.

Then he looked away, snapping the connection, leaving Rebecca feeling even more confused.

Tony made it through dinner by sheer will, certain the simmering attraction that zinged between him and Rebecca was obvious to everyone in the room. This was exactly why having her on staff was such a bad idea. If not for Lea and the kids, he would have taken Rebecca aside after they'd finished eating and told her he'd changed his mind. He wouldn't be able to hire her after all.

But he'd held his tongue. Downed a plate of spaghetti and bowl of salad he'd barely tasted and left Rebecca to get the troops in line for cleanup. Telling her to come to his office when it was time to put Lea to bed, he headed off into the cooling evening to check e-mails and phone messages.

As he dug out a W-4 form and insurance paperwork, he had to admit that Rebecca was as ideal as her résumé had promised. She already had the students well in hand. She'd understood that at eighteen and nineteen years old, this group didn't need an adult wagging her finger at them, treating them like children. She was the boss, just as their future employers would be, but she was compassionate and fair.

The goal of the program was to teach not only the basics for independent living, but to show the kids the ins and outs of the food service business. These six girls and two boys had shown an interest in restaurant work beyond the typical fast-food employment. With Rebecca as a role model, some of them might take the same path as she did—culinary school, then a good job in a top-notch restaurant.

At least that was what Tony had presented to Sam Harrison in the business plan he'd written a year ago. With Rebecca here, he could meet those lofty goals—if he didn't lose his mind in the meantime. If he could shut down the pounding urge to touch her, kiss her, renew every shocking promise he'd made to her in the dark hours of their marriage bed.

It was after eight by the time Rebecca and Lea pushed open his office door. His daughter was flagging, her eyes half-lidded and sleepy as she leaned against Rebecca. Streaks of chocolate bracketed Lea's mouth and competed with the jelly stains on her shirt.

Rebecca sat in the rundown office chair and let Lea collapse against her. "Sorry we're so late. After we finished cleaning up, the kids insisted I show them how to make brownies."

Half-asleep, Lea roused herself to announce, "I like brownies, Daddy."

Rebecca showed him a foil-wrapped package. "Here's your share. I warn you, they're professional strength."

Coming around the desk, he swept up his daughter, settling her head against his shoulder. "Can you grab that paperwork from my desk? Get it filled out tomorrow?"

She picked up the W-4 and insurance form, then followed him outside. "A friend of mine will be subletting the apartment. She said she'd arrange to have my things

shipped." With the sunset, the sky had darkened to midnight blue and a fat crescent moon hung above them. The
cool air drifted on a breeze, carrying the scent of pine and
cedar.

Rebecca opened the door to the main house, then went
inside with him. "Jana told me she's got a bed made up
for me in the guest cottage."

"Good. I'd asked her to do that."

As he started for the stairs, Lea reared her head back.
"Becca has to sleep with me."

One foot on the bottom step, he glanced over his
shoulder. "Rebecca is staying in the cottage with Jana."

Lea shook her head, the set to her mouth uncharacter-
istically obstinate. "With me."

"Your bed's too small, *mija.*"

Rebecca held out her arms for Lea and took her from
him. "Do you know where Jana stays, sweetheart?" Lea
nodded. "Could you find it in the morning when you wake
up? When it's light outside?"

His daughter nodded again as Rebecca started up the
stairs. "That's where I'll be. You can come over as soon
as you get dressed."

"You can't stay with Rebecca all day, *mija,*" Tony said.
"She has work to do."

"But you can help us make breakfast. It has to be light
outside before you come, and you have to ask your daddy
to come with you. Will you do that?"

"I want you to sleep with me," Lea persisted.

Tony moved ahead to Lea's room to show Rebecca the
way. She set his daughter down on the bed's hot-pink
comforter. "My room is right next door, *mija.* You know I
always come when you have bad dreams."

Lea clung to Rebecca's hands. "You won't go away in your car?"

"Absolutely not."

His daughter studied Rebecca's face, wanting to trust the promise. Her mother had broken so many.

Whatever she saw in Rebecca's brown eyes, Lea seemed satisfied. "Will you tuck me in?"

"Sure, sweetheart." Rebecca kissed her forehead.

Tony showed her where Lea's pajamas were, found the tattered blankie Estelle had given to her when she'd been a newborn. Rebecca took her into the bathroom to brush her teeth and wash her face. When they were done, Tony gave Lea three kisses and set a glass of water on the nightstand. He left the small lamp on, its pale yellow glow chasing the worst of the shadows. Elena's photo smiled down from the nightstand.

Lea was asleep almost before he and Rebecca tiptoed from the room. They walked downstairs.

"The guest cottage has a small kitchen," he told her as they crossed the great room. "Jana should have some cereal and milk for breakfast."

"We're making streusel coffee cake. Might as well get started with instruction."

A light shone from the kitchen, that and the one table lamp in the living room the only source of illumination. Where they stood by the front door, the low light seemed to blanket them within an intimate cocoon. With his daughter safely in bed, with he and Rebecca away from the eager eyes of his boisterous students, it seemed anything could happen here, anything was permitted.

They stood only inches apart. He wouldn't touch her. "I couldn't let you stay here in the house. Even for Lea's sake."

"I know."

"Because it wouldn't look right. These kids have seen so much, know far more than kids their age should. But I have to set an example."

She nodded, her gaze lifting to his.

"If you were in the room next door to me…" He broke off, not even wanting to follow that thought. Even if he never put a hand on her, with her as close as his daughter's bedroom, he'd be awake all night. He'd spend the long hours fantasizing about Rebecca.

"I understand," she said.

Then he saw the smear of chocolate on the point of her chin. He should have just told her it was there, let her clean herself up when she got to the cottage. But somehow he was wetting his thumb, was rubbing the spot away. And when he finished the task, his fingers drifted, along the line of her jaw, into the silk of her hair.

Her lips parted as he bent toward her. When he pressed his mouth to hers, it was both coming home and a sizzling new experience. He might have kissed her hundreds of times during their short life together, but none of them quite had the flavor of this one.

She tasted of chocolate and passion. Her skin felt like late nights and smooth sheets. The catch of her breath as his tongue touched her lower lip teased his ears, drove heat down his spine.

He was ready to pull her toward the sofa, to take what he'd never gotten enough of during their short marriage. Might have if her hand hadn't pushed against his chest to separate them.

He stepped away from her. "Damn."

She wouldn't look at him as she gathered the papers and

her purse from the front table. "I'm sorry. I shouldn't have… That was…" One last swift glance at him, and she hurried out the door.

He stood frozen, struggling to knock some sense into his head. Finally he moved out to the porch to watch her make her way toward the cottage. She wasn't likely to encounter anything more dangerous than an early raccoon out here, but he could at least be enough of a gentleman to make sure she got to the cottage okay.

Why the hell had he kissed her? He had more damn self-control than that. He'd better get his head back in the game. Keep in mind what had happened before.

With the sound of the cottage door closing, he went back inside. As he made his way up the stairs, he decided his first order of business would be a shower—the colder the better.

Chapter Four

"Daddy."

Tony snapped awake at the sound of Lea's voice, focusing on her worried face. His gaze strayed to his clock radio, and he stared unbelieving at the time—a quarter after seven, forty-five minutes later than he usually woke. He never set his alarm, didn't need to when his internal clock had its own wake-up call. But after long, sleepless hours replaying in his mind the kiss he'd shared with Rebecca, his body reacting to each remembered moment, he'd fallen into an exhausted slumber near dawn. No wonder he'd overslept.

Lea kept her serious gaze on him as he sat up in bed. "Can we go see Becca?"

"Let me get dressed first, sweetheart." He took in Lea's pajama top stuffed into a pair of denim shorts, the tangle of her hair. "Go change into a clean T-shirt. I'll help you with your ponytail."

Once Lea had hurried off to her own room, Tony shut the door, the signal to his daughter that he needed privacy. He left his door open at night so she could come in anytime if she was afraid. But she would knock first with it shut.

Unbidden, an image arose in his mind of Rebecca in this room with him, swinging the door shut, taking her in his arms. Urging her toward the king-size bed, covering her body with his.

Damn it. That was exactly what had kept him up all night, what had heated his body to a fever pitch. Just when he'd thought he'd banished her from his mind, the images had returned in a rush.

Putting the brakes on his X-rated fantasies, he dragged on blue jeans and a polo shirt embroidered with the Estelle's House logo. Socks and athletic shoes in his hands, he padded down to Lea's room. He found her still in her pajama top. She stood in front of an open dresser drawer contemplating the piles of neatly folded T-shirts.

"Which one, Daddy?"

His heart wrenched at her plaintive question. She'd had so little when she'd been with Elena. The foster mother had handed over a paper market sack with a few pitiful blue jeans, shorts and T-shirts, all of them well-worn. The moment he got Lea home, he'd taken her out, buying her a shopping cart full of new clothes and toys. He'd tried not to go hog wild, didn't want to overwhelm her. But the sight of a drawer filled with clean, nearly new T-shirts still froze her in indecision.

He pulled one out at random. "This one is pretty. Did you change your panties?"

She shook her head solemnly. Taking a pair from the top drawer, he sent her into her bathroom. "Wash your face, too."

He pulled on shoes and socks while he waited. Then, with Lea dressed and her hair neat, they went downstairs. Lea made a beeline for the back door.

Tony stopped her. "You have to have breakfast before we go."

The mulish rebellion in his daughter's face was at once unexpected and welcome. It was the first fight he'd seen in her. "I'm not hungry."

He was tempted to give in, but he knew from experience if his daughter waited too long to eat, she'd be cranky. He doubted she could wait for the coffee cake Rebecca planned for the morning lesson.

"Even still, you have to eat." He turned to the bread basket. "I'll make you some toast. You can take it with you."

Lea wriggled with impatience as he dropped bread in the toaster, then buttered the warm slices. He handed one to her with a napkin, then took a bite of the other. "Let's go."

She nibbled on her toast as she skipped on ahead of him, following the path around his office toward the guest cottage. As they passed the cottage's kitchen window, he saw the curtains hadn't been drawn. He knew it was early yet for Jana—she roused herself at eight for her eight-thirty start time—but could Rebecca still be asleep as well?

The thought of her, warm and slumbering in her bed, wiped everything else from his mind. In that rapt moment of fantasy, his toe caught on a root sent out by a towering black oak across the path. As he stumbled and nearly fell, he could swear the damn tree was laughing at him.

Lea had reached the cottage door and turned to wait for him to catch up. There was still no sign of life from within. Did he take Lea back to the house? Or risk waking Rebecca, having her come to the door sleepy-eyed, hair mussed from her bed?

Lea took the decision out of his hands, knocking on the door. His heart kicked into high speed as footsteps approached, Rebecca's familiar tread. How could he have remembered something as obscure as the way she walked?

To his relief, she was wide awake and dressed for the day, her hair pulled into a ponytail, barrettes holding back the shorter strands. She'd apparently packed work clothes in hopes of getting the job. The businesslike black slacks and short-sleeved white blouse, she wore were about as far from sexy as they could be. Yet even with the shirt buttoned to an inch below her collarbone, his imagination strayed to what was concealed by that plain white fabric. He found himself wondering how easily the buttons would slip from their holes.

Irritated with himself, he shoved his hands into his trouser pockets. "I hope we're not too early."

"She could have come over earlier. I've been up awhile." She bent to accept Lea's cautious hug, one silky lock of hair escaping her barrette. When she straightened, she lifted her hands to corral the escapee, the graceful lines of her arms drawing Tony's gaze.

He looked away, back down the path. "I have paperwork and phone calls this morning, but I'll be over at the kitchen this afternoon."

"Am I on probation?" He turned back to her to see her smiling.

Just the sight of that gentle curve of her lips lifted a

weight inside him. But damn it, he didn't want her to make him feel good. "I have to be sure, Rebecca." He injected cool neutrality into his tone. "I can't make any missteps with these kids. They've been let down too many times in their lives."

Something flickered in her eyes. Guilt? Because of the way she'd let him down when she left eleven years ago? He ought to feel vindicated by that look of pain, but instead he just wanted to pull her in his arms as he had last night.

His body responded instantly, and he felt heat rise in his face. And she saw it.

Lea leaning against her, Rebecca lowered her voice. "About what happened—"

"It was a mistake, Rebecca." He glanced down at his daughter. She was watching the antics of a squirrel in the black oak. "One that we won't be repeating."

She lifted her chin. "Of course not."

He crouched to eye level with Lea. "You can spend an hour with Rebecca, then I'll send Jana over to bring you back to the house."

He saw the flash of rebellion again and wondered if his complacent daughter would defy him. But she just sighed, accepting his hug.

As he rose, Rebecca's fragrance drifted toward him. He nearly leaned closer to seek out its source. Instead he backed away, banging his elbow on the gnarled truck of the black oak. "Call over to my office if there's a problem." He retreated down the gravel path.

In his office, he cranked up the AC, then stood in front of the vent to let the chilled air wash over him. It was only in the high seventies out there this time of the morning, but it felt like a hundred with Rebecca in the vicinity. If he didn't grow up, stop acting like a randy adolescent, he'd be making another mistake with his ex-wife like the one he made last night.

He just wouldn't think of her. Planting himself in his chair, he pulled his to-do list toward him and scanned it. He'd just reached for the phone to make his first call of the morning when movement outside his office window caught his eye. Rebecca and Lea walked toward the bakeshop, Rebecca's hips softly swaying in those austere black slacks.

Tony's mouth went dry as he watched her, concealed and then revealed as she moved amongst the trees that lined the path. Even when she'd disappeared inside the bakeshop kitchen, it took him ten distracted minutes to clear his mind enough to settle back to work.

The moods of Rebecca's charges as they wandered into the bakeshop more or less by the eight o'clock start time ran the gamut from Katy's cheerfulness to Serena's sullenness to Ruby's sleepy inattentiveness. Kevin initially refused to don the required hairnet over his goatee, spitting out an expletive that cost him a quarter in the cuss jar. James spent the first twenty minutes hitting on Colleen, and Ari barely spoke to anyone.

Used to the varying degrees of commitment she'd encountered in food-service employees, Rebecca wasn't fazed by Serena's early morning crankiness or Brittany's standoffishness. She just gave each one a task, telling them firmly the job was their responsibility and no one would do it for them.

At least the circus of the first half hour or so kept her mind off Tony and her immediate reaction when she'd opened the door to him this morning. If not for Lea, Rebecca would have stared at him, moon-eyed, swamped by memories of their kiss. The little girl's presence acted as a much-needed buffer, a deterrent to the impulse that had rushed through Rebecca's mind—to reach for Tony, see if his skin still felt as warm as it had last night, see if his scent still rocked her to her core.

Rebecca had teamed Lea with Ruby to make the streusel for the coffee cake. Sitting on a kitchen stool and wearing latex gloves far too large for her small hands, Lea squished together softened butter, brown sugar, flour and cinnamon. Beside her, Ruby chopped the walnuts that would also go into the topping.

On the other side of the kitchen, Brittany, James and Ari were working on the batter. While butter and sugar creamed in the floor mixer, Brittany cracked eggs into a two-quart measure. James readied the buttermilk, and Ari portioned out flour, salt and baking soda. Kevin was greasing and flouring cake pans while Colleen lined them with parchment paper. Cheerful Katy, a self-declared math hater, was in the dining room, moaning and groaning over a calculator as she toted up the cost of the recipe's ingredients, a task the others had completed last night.

Batter and streusel topping ready, the eight ten-inch round cake pans went into the ovens and Rebecca put half the group onto cleanup crew and two on setup in the dining room. She assigned Serena to help Katy, still struggling with the calculator. While the buttermilk streusel cakes neared the finish line in the oven, filling the air with their spicy perfume, Rebecca gathered everyone around Katy, ready to launch into a quick lesson in pricing.

"This is impossible," Katy exclaimed, pushing the calculator away. "What does it matter?"

Before she could draw breath to answer, Tony's deep voice cut in. "We're here to make a profit, Katy." He strode from the kitchen into the dining room. "How will you know how much to charge for a slice of coffee cake if you don't know what it cost you to make?"

Glaring at Tony over Katy's head, Rebecca put a hand on Tony's arm. "Could I speak with you a moment?"

With her students an avid audience, Rebecca pulled Tony toward the side door to the dining room. When Lea would have followed, Rebecca told her, "Stay with Ruby, sweetheart."

Under her hand, his muscle flexed, larger and more powerful than what she remembered twelve years ago. Instinctually she wanted to memorize its feel, explore its texture. The moment the door to the bakeshop shut behind them, she let go and confronted him.

"Who's in charge here?" she asked. "You or me?"

"This is my program."

"But this is my kitchen. How can I maintain authority if you interrupt me in the middle of a lesson?"

He stared down at her, his face expressionless. He'd perfected that emotional barrier during his years in foster care, a trick Rebecca hadn't had time to learn.

He dipped his head in a brief nod. "I apologize."

"Thank you." She glanced back through the windows. Colleen was chasing James around the dining room, the other teens focused on them. "You know I respect what you're doing here. But these kids are as loosey-goosey as a herd of cats. They have to trust that I know what I'm talking about without your intervention."

"I agree." His deep voice rumbled in her ear, hypnotic. "Then we should go back in."

Except he didn't move, his body between her and the door. The shade of the overhanging oaks and pines doused the rising heat of late morning. A light breeze curled against her cheek. Her skin felt alive and sensitive, as if the slightest touch would shatter her into a million pieces.

Tony loomed over her, his dark eyes smoldering. He seemed as helpless to look away as she. She knew if they didn't go back inside, didn't sever the invisible, white-hot link between them, the teens would notice, would come out to check on them. Yet she felt transfixed by him, as if she were caught in a time shift between past and present.

"Rebecca…" Her murmured name stroked her like a caress. She took a step closer.

The door swung open, and Ruby poked her head out. "The timer's dinging."

Rebecca edged past Tony and went inside. On the way to the kitchen, she called out, "James, Colleen, quit the horseplay, grab a pair of oven mitts." She gestured at the boy and girl to follow her. "Kevin, we need cooling racks on the island. Ari, show him where they are."

Opening the oven, she used a mitt to tug out the top shelf. The wave of heat that roiled out was familiar, comforting. Not like the unsettling fire that had blazed between her and Tony.

"Press your finger lightly near the center," she told the watching crew. All but Katy had followed her into the kitchen; a glance out into the dining room told her that Tony was with her. "If it feels springy, it's done." Once the cakes were safely on the cooling racks, she'd have the others try the test.

As she supervised the ferrying of the hot pans from ovens to racks, her gaze strayed to Tony, patiently running through the numbers with Katy. While she would have preferred to do that task with the girl, she appreciated Tony's help.

Just seeing his broad back, the muscles playing in his shoulders as he shifted in his chair, she wanted to go to him. To curve her arms around him and hold him close. The way she did a dozen years ago, when they were so young and so in love.

Her mind snapped back to the here and now with Serena's plaintive query. "When do we eat? I'm starving."

The others chimed in, as eager as Serena to cut into the coffee cakes. "They're too hot," Rebecca told them. "You'll have nothing but crumbs on your plate."

Katy let loose a triumphant cry, the cost-analysis task apparently finally sinking in. She hurried to the kitchen, Tony at her heels. Arms crossed over his chest, he propped a shoulder against the doorway between the kitchen and dining room. His steady gaze on Rebecca stole her breath.

She forced a smile. "I suppose you're hungry, too."

The hunger in his eyes answered for him. "I could eat."

She turned away, focusing back on the noisy crowd of teens. "We can divvy up two of the cakes and let the others cool."

The pandemonium increased as the students went in several directions at once, gathering serving utensils, plates and forks. Lea stayed close to her dad while Katy hurried out to the bunkhouse and cottage to summon Estelle and Jana for breakfast. Rebecca served up the coffee cake, most of the servings falling into soft, warm crumbs, while the students carried plates out to the dining-room table.

The teens had butted the two tables up together and made sure Estelle had the place of honor at one end. Tony took the other end. Rebecca intended to sit beside Estelle, as far away from Tony as she could. But by the time she returned from washing the sticky crumbs from her hands, the only chair left was the one right beside him, opposite Lea.

The ravenous teens were so busy wolfing down the fragrant coffee cake, they didn't see her stop short in the kitchen doorway. Only Tony noticed, his gaze meeting hers across the room. He rose, pulling out her chair. When she saw he wouldn't sit until she did, she got her feet moving, keeping her focus on the chair instead of Tony.

Once they were both seated, positioned at right angles to one another, she tried to keep from touching him. But their knees brushed despite her efforts, each brief contact setting off heat inside her. Yet while Rebecca's stomach tightened into knots, Tony seemed oblivious, his expression unchanged as he smiled down at his daughter.

"Do you like your coffee cake, *mija?*"

Lea nodded, her mouth full. "Can I have some more?"

"If it's okay with Rebecca." He looked her way, his gaze impassive.

Crossing her legs and edging away from Tony, Rebecca addressed the table. "Anyone ready for seconds?"

"I'd love some," Estelle said, pushing to her feet.

"I'll bring you some, Grams," Kevin called out. "You don't have to get up."

When Rebecca would have risen to help, Tony pressed her back down with a hand on her shoulder. "Let them do it."

He was right, of course, but his touch fogged her mind.

She shrugged away from the contact. "Go ahead and cut into a third pan," she told Kevin. "You might need smaller portions for the second go-round. Ari, you and Ruby give him a hand."

The teens swarmed into the kitchen, Lea flitting amongst them, eager for her second piece of cake. They served Estelle and Tony, but Rebecca passed on another wedge. She'd barely eaten any of the first slice.

She forced herself to eat, mechanically analyzing the crumb and texture, the level of sweetness and balance of spices. Rather than entertain the memories that flashed in her mind—her body tangled with Tony's, the friction of warm skin against skin—she directed her thoughts toward the mundane. Fewer walnuts and more cinnamon in the recipe, slightly less sugar and a splash more buttermilk. Anything to cope with the turbulence in her mind.

Yet where she could think of nothing but touching him, feeling his warmth, Tony seemed completely unmoved by her. He barely looked her way as he ate, instead chiding Lea to take another sip of milk, laughing at a silly joke James told. Their kiss last night, with its passion and heat, might never have happened.

Finally breakfast was over, and Rebecca could put some space between her and Tony. She divided the teens up into teams for final cleanup and packaging of the remaining five cakes. Six slices from each pan, each one wrapped in plastic wrap and stashed in the freezer. A quick consultation—which Rebecca made sure included Katy—to agree on the price per piece. Another run through the recipe, with Rebecca explaining the adjustments she'd decided on.

Inexplicably, Tony didn't return to his office after breakfast. He sent Lea off with Jana, but he stayed behind.

Out of the way of the bustle of the kitchen, seated on a stool by the door, he might as well have been shadowing Rebecca's every step. She could barely breathe with him there, had to struggle for coherent thought.

Finally, after they'd agreed to meet for lunch and quiche Lorraine, the group dispersed. Still Tony lingered, holding open the door for her as she exited the kitchen. He locked the door, then walked beside her.

"Was there something else?" she asked, feeling unsettled. "I have lesson plans to prepare."

He shoved his hands into his pockets. "I need to get a key to the bakeshop made for you. I should have before now, but haven't had the time."

"Estelle gave me hers."

"That's good. Until I can get another made."

They'd reached his office, where Rebecca thought they'd part company. She needed to get away from him, to recover her equilibrium. But he continued on past the small structure that served as his office.

Rebecca stopped in the shade of an oak tree. "You might not need to talk about this, but I do. I'm sorry I kissed you last night. Sorry I touched you. It brought up too much…"

She shook her head slowly. "I can't brush it under the carpet like you can. I know you feel nothing for me anymore, I know what we had before is dead. That's exactly the way it should be. I want you to know I have no intention of starting anything up with you. That me kissing you was just…an aberration. A mistake, like you said."

His silence weighed heavily on her. She felt exposed and raw, a little angry that he wouldn't speak. Finally, she broke away from him, hurrying off toward the guest cottage, feeling his gaze on her every step of the way.

Chapter Five

Two hours later, Tony stared at his computer screen, the words of the Estelle's House business plan a blur. Guilt still burned in his gut at how his silence had wounded Rebecca. Despite his lingering bitterness over her leaving him eleven years ago, she didn't deserve to be treated so shabbily.

She'd laid herself bare to him out there on the path, and he hadn't said a word. He'd let her believe their kiss last night was her fault, that she'd made a move on him instead of the other way around. That he'd felt nothing, rather than the explosion that still reverberated inside him.

Her honesty had torn her up—he could see it in her eyes. But he'd acted the coward, holding his tongue when he should have clarified that *he* had made the first move. The whole damn thing had been *his* fault. And he would do it again in a heartbeat if he didn't know how huge a mistake that would be.

He'd seen her walk by a half hour ago, headed back to the bakeshop for lunch prep. The students were just starting to trickle in, arriving singly or in pairs. James hovered over Colleen as if she were a star fallen from heaven, his head with its blond Mohawk dipping down as he whispered in her ear.

Tony jumped at the knock on his office door. He hadn't seen anyone approach through the window, but his heart kicked into overdrive nevertheless. Even though it couldn't be Rebecca—she was still in the bakeshop—his body responded in anticipation.

The door opened, and Estelle stepped inside. "Am I interrupting anything?"

"I was just watching young love," Tony said, nodding in the direction of James and Colleen, who lingered outside the bakeshop.

Estelle watched them a moment through the open door, then swung it shut. "About the same age as you and Rebecca."

When we fell in love. Rebecca had been eighteen, same age as Colleen, Tony twenty, a year older than James. For years, Tony and Becca had been only friends. Then friendship sparked into something different.

Through the window, he saw James hold the door for Colleen, and the two of them disappeared inside. Tony gestured to the chair opposite his desk. "Did you want to talk to me about something?"

Estelle eased herself into the worn office chair, looking stiff and tired. Tony jumped to his feet. "Why don't you take my seat. It's more comfortable."

"I'm only sixty-three. I don't need you treating me like

an old lady." She shifted, wincing. "My back has just been a little sore lately."

Tony returned to his chair, not liking the shadows under Estelle's eyes. "Is there an issue with one of the kids?" he asked again.

She shook her head. "Just wondering what you thought of Becca."

Was his preoccupation so obvious? Had his foster mother seen the heat that had flashed between him and Rebecca during breakfast? Every time her knees brushed against his, it had been all he could do to keep from reaching for her, kissing her again in front of that eager audience.

He scrambled to muster a response. He'd never been able to lie to Estelle all those years he lived with her. She'd suss out an untruth in an instant, leaving honesty as his only refuge.

His foster mother's gaze sharpened on him. "I mean, do you think Becca's a good match for our students?"

He tried to stop the flush from rising in his cheeks, but was certain Estelle saw it anyway. "She's doing well with them. She's knowledgeable. Fair but firm."

"Good. I'm glad to hear you're giving her a chance."

"I had to because of Lea," he reminded her. "You could have warned me. Let me know before the interview that it was Becca."

"If you'd known, would you have agreed to the interview?"

Under her piercing stare, he shook his head.

Estelle linked her hands in her lap. They looked swollen, something Tony hadn't noticed before. Likely from the summer's fierce heat.

"I know you're still angry, Tony," Estelle said, her

fingers shifting. "But before you and Becca married, you were friends."

"She calls herself Rebecca now," Tony said. A trivial matter, but the name change allowed him to pretend this woman wasn't the same one with whom he'd fallen so deeply in love.

"You two were thick as thieves once," Estelle said, a trace of reverie in her tone.

And then she stole my heart.

They'd bonded immediately when she'd first arrived at Estelle's. Becca had been grief stricken, terrified for her parents; he was still mourning the death of his mother at his father's hands. The entire year Becca spent there, they'd been inseparable.

She'd turned ten in foster care, had received twenty dollars in birthday money from her financially pressed parents. Two months later she'd spent nearly all that money on a CD Tony had been coveting. That and a new shirt and blue jeans from Estelle had been the only gifts he'd received for his twelfth birthday.

Three months after that, Becca returned to her parents. Tony transformed into a monster—he was still apologizing to Estelle for that—too angry and confused to understand what he was feeling. His anger frightened him.

Only after he understood that Becca wasn't lost to him, that she intended to continue their friendship as soon as her life back home settled down, did that blackness lift. She'd been a spark of joy throughout his foster childhood.

Then came the tipping point, when everything changed between him and Becca. When the skinny, awkward girl blossomed into a mysterious woman. When one night's mistake changed their lives forever.

Estelle drew him from his reverie. "I'd hoped you could be friends again."

"No." He paused, then softened his sharp tone. "We'd be better off with a business relationship." Because with Rebecca, friendship was just one inadvertent touch away from intimacy.

Estelle pushed to her feet, swaying slightly. Again, worry twinged inside him. "Are you coming over for lunch?" she asked.

"Have Jana bring me over something." He didn't feel ready to wade back into the landmine that was Rebecca.

Estelle left, and he rose to watch her walk toward the bakeshop. Her purposeful stride eased his anxiety. Maybe she just hadn't slept well. Her hearing was sharper than any watchdog's, and if the kids were up to any mischief during the night, it would have roused her.

She'd certainly caught him and Becca often enough the year Becca lived there and later when she'd spend the night. They'd thought they were being oh so quiet creeping down the halls past her bedroom and out to the back porch. They only wanted to talk, reveal to each other their childish hopes and fears, to find some answer to the future in the black night sky filled with stars. But when they sneaked back into the kitchen, Estelle was always there, nursing a cup of tea, waiting for him and Becca to come back inside.

He'd had to apologize to his foster mom for that, too. Despite the innocence of those nights, he'd broken Estelle's rules. She didn't have to say a word as she watched them tiptoe to their beds. Tony assigned himself a punishment—another night of doing dishes or raking the knee-deep elm leaves from the front lawn. But he didn't stop meeting Becca on the back porch.

His stomach rumbled, urging him to follow the path and join the others in the bakeshop. He ignored its complaints, turning back to his computer and the work waiting for him.

After that first morning, Rebecca saw little of Tony. Other than dropping Lea off at the guest cottage before breakfast, he seemed to make a point of keeping a buffer of a half-dozen or so teens between him and her. At meal-times, he'd grab a quick bite of whatever Rebecca and the students were preparing for the day, usually wolfing it down in the kitchen before heading back to his office or the main house.

"He's satisfied with your work," Estelle told her when Rebecca wondered aloud at his absence. "He doesn't need to supervise you every minute of the day."

Of course he didn't. And there was no reason to feel as if something was missing from her day when he didn't sit with the group to share a meal or stay behind to help with cleanup. As off-kilter as he made her feel, wasn't it better that he made himself scarce?

Yet his absence increased the tension between them rather than lessening it. Electricity seemed to crackle between them on the rare ocassions when he was near. One afternoon as they cleaned up from lunch, she caught him watching her from across the kitchen, his intense dark brown gaze as palpable as a touch. Her entire focus centered on that visual connection, and it took Ruby shouting her name to pull Rebecca from her daze.

By Friday, Rebecca's rowdy group of teens was stir-crazy and ready for something different. After dinner, everyone gathered in the bunkhouse for a movie, Tony included. Halfway through the action adventure film,

James and Kevin exchanged heated words and nearly got physical with one another. It took Tony to break them apart. Colleen broke into tears and ran to her room, Ruby got into Kevin's face and told him he was a jerk and Lea had a meltdown at the ruckus.

It took Rebecca and Jana both to soothe Lea enough that Jana could carry her off to the house and bed. With the boys on opposite sofas in the bunkhouse living room, Tony ordered them to hash out their problems without resorting to violence. It was midnight before the boys and later the girls got the air cleared, dragging up everything from Serena's claim that Ruby stole her toothpaste to Ari's resurgent grief over the recent loss of her younger brother to drugs.

Instinct told Rebecca this was Tony's domain, and she stepped back to let him work. He knew the questions to ask to get at the source of Kevin's anger—Colleen had been his girlfriend before they'd moved to Estelle's House—and knew what to say to ease the pain of Kevin's wounded pride. He told Serena he'd bring by a permanent marker to identify her things and he encouraged the girls to sit with Ari while Rebecca fetched a box of tissues for her tears.

When they'd all quieted, one or two looking ready to fall asleep, Tony took Rebecca aside. "Had you planned an early start tomorrow? Because I don't know if this crew could handle it."

"I can switch gears." She turned to the sleepy teens. "Let's meet at ten o'clock. We'll have an easy day tomorrow."

Bleary-eyed, they rose and drifted off to their rooms. Rebecca gave Estelle a hug good-night, then walked out into the cool darkness.

Tony followed, walking alongside her on the gravel path. The waning half-moon barely lit the path. With Jana at the house with Lea, the guest cottage was dark.

As they moved along, Tony's arm would brush hers, his skin warm and familiar. She should have forgotten what his touch felt like long before now.

When they reached the cottage, she turned to him. "I have an idea, but I'll need your help. How many can you transport in your Suburban?"

"Seven total."

"That should work. I have seating for five in my car."

"Where are we going?" he asked, his smile a slash of white in the dark. He leaned in close, sandwiching her between the cottage door and his warm body.

"The farmer's market in Placerville," she told him. "If that's okay. If you can take the morning off."

"Sure." Still only inches away from her, he bent his head down. "There's something I need to tell you. What I should have told you days ago."

He wasn't touching her, but sensation fingered its way up her spine. She could barely gather breath to speak. "What's that?"

"What you said about things being dead between us." She heard a hard edge to the words. "The past is gone. We can't get it back. But when I kissed you—"

"But I—" His hand covered her mouth.

"When *I* kissed *you*...that was on me. I don't want to revisit old history anymore than you do, but I..." He looked away. "I let myself forget that. Just for a moment. My fault. Not yours."

With that, he turned on his heel and strode away along

the path. Her thoughts chaotic, her heart thundering in her ears, it took Rebecca a full minute to open the door and slip inside.

Lea had a bad night, waking up crying around three in the morning, terrified by a nightmare she could barely remember. Nearly an hour later she finally fell asleep again in Tony's arms as he sat propped up in her narrow twin bed. He woke bad-tempered, with the mother of all stiff necks. It didn't help that when he walked out to the parking lot and saw Rebecca standing amongst the group of teens, all he could think about was her fingers massaging the pain away.

Then Lea not only refused to leave his side, she didn't want Rebecca out of her sight either. When he confided in Rebecca and Estelle about Lea's nightmares, they managed to find a compromise. They asked Ruby to drive Rebecca's Corolla, allowing Lea to ride with both her father and Rebecca. Then it took a good ten minutes for the eight teens to decide who would ride in which vehicle. Tony let them handle it, intervening only to put James and Colleen in the middle seat row of the Suburban with Lea between them. A futile effort to keep the two of them apart. At the least, it might slow them down.

Finally, at ten-thirty, they all waved goodbye to Jana and started down the hill to the farmer's market. With the day off, Jana had her own plans with her boyfriend, Ian.

Lea, still fragile from her night terrors, leaned forward in her seat, small arm outstretched to hold Rebecca's hand. It was awkward for Rebecca and sheer torture for Tony. Rebecca had to twist her body around and lie halfway across the console. It meant her caramel-streaked hair brushed against his arm, and her fragrance teased his nose.

He could have positioned his body more toward the door, eked out an inch of space between him and Rebecca. But it felt so damn good having her that close. He could so easily indulge himself by letting his forearm rest against her rib cage, feel the slip and slide of her silky shirt against her body.

Finally, Rebecca straightened, Lea satisfied by James and Colleen's promise to hold her hand. An excuse for them to link their own fingers, but if it comforted his daughter, he wouldn't complain.

Damn, but he wanted to reach for her as Lea had, rest their hands together on the console between them. But they had an audience of five in the Suburban. What in the world would he tell them? That every time he was with her, he couldn't resist touching her, breathing in her scent? That he wanted to relive the past, those moments in the dark when passion had overwhelmed them?

He kept his hands on the steering wheel as they wound their way down the back roads into Placerville. It had been a hotter than usual July and the first day of August wasn't proving to be any cooler. The hillsides they passed, alternately filled with wine vineyards and the spruces and firs of Christmas tree farms, shimmered in the glare of the midmorning sun.

In Placerville, Tony parked the truck beside Rebecca's Corolla and the teens piled out of the vehicles. Across Main Street, the farmer's market had been set up in a parking lot, rows of stalls filled with local produce and teeming with customers. Most of his group were city kids from Sacramento. Living on a ranch was enough of a mind-bender for them. The farmer's market would be another introduction to a different world.

"Stay close to me," Rebecca told them as they crossed the street.

The teens crowded around her like chicks following their mother. He could barely see Lea clinging to Rebecca's hand like a lifeline. He and Estelle brought up the rear as they started down the first row of stalls.

Rebecca's voice carried over the surrounding clamor. "The kind of produce you'll find will vary depending on the time of year. Unlike the supermarket that transports fruits and vegetables from around the world, everything here is grown locally. You'll only find what's in season."

They stopped at a stand selling strawberries so vividly red they looked unreal. The teens descended on the samples set in a basket up front. After handing a fat strawberry to Lea, Rebecca bit into her own, scarlet juice wetting her lips. Tony couldn't care less about the cool berry in his hand; he wanted to lick and taste from Rebecca's mouth.

He turned away to find Estelle's sharp gaze on him. "Strolling down memory lane?"

Damn, he was blushing. He felt like a twelve-year-old again under Estelle's regard. "That would be a wasted trip," he told her as he tasted his sample. It was sugar-sweet and tart all at once.

"And not one to be taken lightly," Estelle said with a glance down at Lea.

"I'm not twenty anymore. I have better sense than that."

They continued on down the row; Rebecca identifying items that weren't familiar to her students. Kale and kohlrabi, rutabagas and leeks. Chinese cabbage and kumquats.

She explained from what family each fruit or vegetable came and what dish they might use it in.

At first, Lea seemed overwhelmed by the number of people, the noise, the myriad smells and tastes. But as they went along, she grew braver, pointing out new discoveries in the stalls ahead. When she spotted a booth selling brownies and cookies, she all but hauled Rebecca over to it.

"Daddy, come taste," Lea called out to him.

Rebecca set a small square of brownie in his hand, her fingertips ever so lightly stoking his palm as she did so. The touch was unintentional and meant nothing; she did the same when she handed a tidbit to Estelle. But the sensation lingered along his skin, tangling with the rich taste of chocolate.

"Can we get some?" Katy asked, eyeing the piles of oatmeal raisin and chocolate chip cookies.

"What do you think, Katy?" Rebecca asked. "Buy cookies or make them ourselves?"

"Buying them would be easier," Katy said.

"But look how much they cost," Ruby protested. "We could make them way cheaper."

Katy put her hands to her blond head. "Please don't ask me to figure that out. My brain will explode."

They all laughed, Katy included. Rebecca cut them loose to explore the market on their own, and they took off in twos and threes.

Estelle, with a wink, bought a dozen cookies. "For sampling." Then, with a bribe of tastes, she took Lea's hand and wandered off into the crowd.

Rebecca watched her go. "Does Lea have many bad nights like last night?"

"Not like the first couple weeks. Neither one of us got much sleep then."

Rebecca moved along the aisle to a booth selling almonds and walnuts. "She didn't like the boys fighting."

"She didn't like the yelling." Tony picked up a bag of raw almonds, set it down again, unsure of what to do with his hands. He only knew he had to keep them off Rebecca. "I have to be careful what she watches on television. The few times I've had to discipline her, I learned pretty quickly to do it in a quiet voice."

Rebecca selected a bag of jalapeño-flavored pistachios. "Did her mother yell at her?"

He shook his head. "The only time Elena was loud was when she was laughing. I never heard her raise her voice to Lea."

The pistachios paid for, Rebecca stuffed them away in the large canvas bag she carried. "Someone else, then."

"No way of knowing who. Social services in Reno said the foster care was excellent. I met the woman—she seemed nice enough. I don't know about Elena's friends, the people she might have had babysitting her."

They continued up the next aisle. "What if I help you put her to bed? Maybe read her a story, tuck her in?"

It might help Lea, but how would he deal with the intimacy of having Rebecca in his home every night? Even though she would leave to sleep in the cottage, how would he banish her from his mind when he took to his own bed?

Still, he was a grownup and his daughter had to come first. "There were a few children's books at Elena's house when social services took custody of Lea. They gave them to me with the rest of her things." That half-filled paper bag had been a sharp reminder of his own days as a foster child. "I've bought her some others since then. I think Lea would enjoy having you read them."

Up ahead, partially concealed between a stall selling fresh salmon and a juice stand, James and Colleen were embracing. The boy leaned down to kiss Colleen, the two of them apparently oblivious to curious passersby.

"What do you intend to do about that?" Rebecca asked.

"They're both adults. I'm not their father. They know the rules." Which only applied at the ranch. Neither one had a car, but if they were to sweet talk Jana into lending hers....

Rebecca watched as James curved his arm around Colleen and drew her from their hiding place. "Do you remember..." Her gaze met Tony's, her mouth curved in a gentle smile.

It all came back in a rush. When they were eighteen and twenty, their first stolen kisses at midnight, hidden in the shadows on Estelle's back porch. Becca in his arms, the wonder of tastes and sounds and scents.

She looked away, her smile fading. "We should get going. Could you help me gather up the troops?"

Once they had the scattered teens collected, Rebecca quickly took them through the market to make her final purchases—leeks and kohlrabi, red-leaf lettuce, orange and yellow heirloom tomatoes, purple bell peppers. She also purchased a flat of strawberries and a box of Elberta peaches.

They walked back to the cars, nearly everyone loaded down with a crate, box or bag. Before she climbed into the Corolla, Estelle parceled out the cookies, suggesting they share so they could try all three varieties she'd bought.

As they waited their turn to pull out of the parking lot, Rebecca broke hers and Tony's cookies in half so they could each sample chocolate chip and oatmeal raisin. The pieces in her lap, she bit into hers, the motion of her mouth enchanting. A crumb clung to her lower lip, and before he could stop himself, he reached over and brushed it away with his thumb. Then he couldn't seem to break the contact.

"Tony." She almost whispered his name.

He was ready to reach across the console for her when a horn honked. The driver in the minivan behind them waved an impatient hand. Tony pulled out, keeping his eyes resolutely on the road in front of him.

Chapter Six

The first week of August broke a record for consecutive hundred-degree-plus days down in the Sacramento Valley. The ranch's elevation above three thousand feet moderated the broiling temperatures the city dwellers endured, but for Rebecca, used to much more temperate L.A., the nineties were plenty warm.

The heat impacted the teens as well, exacerbating hair-trigger tempers. Serena and Ari, already suspicious and standoffish with Rebecca, grew more surly and rude each day. More than once, they outright refused to perform a task Rebecca had given them, preferring to sit in the dining room and gossip about the other girls. Rebecca had seen Katy and Colleen in tears more than once over the backbiting. Only Ruby, reserved but straightforward and honest, and uncomplicated Brittany seemed to have their heads in the game.

By Friday night, Rebecca was relieved to have her duties with the fractious teens finished for the day. At eight-thirty, the night air had grown balmy and the valley's delta breeze had made its way up into the foothills. As she hurried to the main house, a silky breeze caressed her skin, heightening her anticipation of seeing Tony.

Because he ate breakfast and dinner in the main house and Jana brought his lunch to his office, Rebecca scarcely saw him. The few minutes that they visited before he took her up to Lea were a brightness carved out of a hectic and sometimes disheartening day.

He was waiting for her on the front porch, head tipped up to watch the darkening sky. In Hawaiian shirt and jeans, the pale glow of the porch light softening his face, he was twenty again. Her heart ached seeing him.

When he saw her, he turned away to open the screen door. "How'd it go today?"

Rebecca made a face as she climbed the stairs. "Not as productive as I would have liked. Half the time the girls are in tears. The rest of the time they're at each other's throats."

He stepped aside to let her enter. "I guess the honeymoon is over."

She laughed. "We passed that point a week ago."

"Anything I can do?"

"Not really." She followed him up to the second floor. "For the most part, I think they respect me. And I don't let them get away with much."

"They're scared to death of what comes next. Sometimes that fear explodes into emotional outbursts."

"I know. But sometimes they make it worse for themselves."

As she herself did, Rebecca realized as she walked along the landing behind Tony. The more time she spent here at the ranch, the more emotional confusion piled up. Want, need, longing tangled inside her. She knew it was only because of what he and Lea represented to her, the way their mere presence stirred up the past. But it nevertheless unsettled her, made her wish for something she didn't even understand.

He entered his daughter's bedroom. "Becca's here, sweetheart."

Nestled in her bed, her dark hair still damp from her bath, Lea reached for Rebecca. As she wrapped her arms around the little girl, Rebecca's soul seemed to fill until she thought it would burst from the sweetness.

She pulled away, swallowing back tears. "I see you've got the books ready." *Green Eggs and Ham, The Very Hungry Caterpillar* and *Goodnight, Moon* were already stacked on the nightstand.

"Can you read them all?" Lea asked.

"Sure, sweetheart. Give Daddy a good-night hug and kiss."

Tony leaned over to take his daughter in his arms. When he tried to draw back, Lea clutched his hand. "Stay, Daddy. Stay and hear the stories this time."

Tony glanced over at Rebecca, and she could feel the heat in his gaze. She knew why he went downstairs or to his own room during story time. Even with his daughter there, a thread of sensual tension grew taut between them in the close confines of Lea's room. If their hearts had given up on the past, if their minds were convinced that there was no longer anything between them, their bodies had refused to get the message.

"I'll stay for a little while, *mija*. Then there's some work I have to do." He moved to stand in the doorway. Rebecca saw the tightness in his body as he leaned against the jamb.

Lea scooted over, making room for Rebecca. She slipped off her shoes as she always did, stretching out on the bed. She took *Green Eggs and Ham* from the stack.

Lea snuggled under her arm, turning the pages as Rebecca read them, the story already memorized. Lea would sometimes point to a picture, ask, "What's that?" They were the same questions she asked every night, as if she needed to be reassured the answers were the same.

As Lea glued herself even more tightly against her, Rebecca realized she was lost. She'd completely fallen in love with Tony's daughter, had built a home for her inside that would never be filled by anyone else. She'd known the risk the moment she first met Lea, and the days and nights spent with her had only made matters worse.

As Lea turned a page, Rebecca gave Tony a sidelong glance. The expression on his face, the naked love she saw there, hit her heart like a hammer. Of course he loved his daughter—what else would she expect? But to see so much devotion pouring from him just made the ache inside her that much harder to bear.

She'd survived the death of her son, the loss of the foster daughter she'd hoped to adopt. She would endure Lea's passing out of her life. She would be strong enough because she had to be.

"Becca?" Lea's small voice pulled her back to the present. Rebecca bent her head and continued to read.

Rebecca all but dragged herself from bed the next morning, exhausted by a bad night's sleep after leaving

Tony and Lea. She wasn't looking forward to their planned trip to the farmer's market, which would no doubt be accompanied by the usual sniping and truculence.

Starting the day off on the wrong foot, Kevin sank into a sullen silence during the drive, shooting dark looks James's way every time the other boy kissed Colleen. They made it through the farmer's market without incident, but later that afternoon, the kitchen's simmering heat seemed to give the boys the excuse to escalate their bickering. Hoping to separate them, Rebecca sent Kevin out with Brittany to set up the dining room for dinner.

Focused on demonstrating preparation of a white sauce, Rebecca didn't see James slip out into the dining room. Shouted, angry words were her first warning of trouble. By the time she tossed out an order to turn off the flame under the white sauce and hurried from the kitchen, James and Kevin's verbal parry had escalated into a physical confrontation.

Kevin, taller and heavier than James, knocked the smaller boy to the floor. Shouting in rage, Kevin pounded James while Colleen screamed.

"Get Tony!" Rebecca shouted at Ruby.

As the other girls looked on in horror, Rebecca ran back into the kitchen, grabbing a pot at random. Filling it with cold water, she carried it out to the dining room where the boys knocked aside chairs as they rolled on the floor. With a heave, she dumped the cold water on them.

They sprang apart with a bellow, James's gelled Mohawk plastered to his head, Kevin's dark brown buzz cut dripping. Colleen crouched beside James, holding a wad of paper napkins to his bloody nose. Kevin got to his feet, and from the look on his face, Rebecca could see the cold water hadn't cooled his anger.

He rounded on Rebecca, closing the distance between them. The boy's height exceeded her own five foot six by at least eight inches, and despite his skinny, nineteen-year-old's frame, he was still big. Rebecca felt a flutter of fear, but knew the last thing she should do was back down.

"Sit down, Kevin." She kept her voice even.

He seemed to draw himself up taller. "I don't have to do what you tell me."

"Sit," Rebecca repeated.

Rebecca could see him waver between his rage and his frail but growing respect for her. His big feet were planted almost toe to toe with hers, and his hands were raised and tightened into fists. She could see his skinned knuckles, still red with the blood that hadn't been washed off by the water.

Serena and Ari, standing with Colleen and the others, shouted out warnings. "Knock it off, Kevin." "Don't do it, man."

She held her ground, keeping her gaze fixed on Kevin's. She knew the boy didn't want to hurt her, but she also knew a little of his history that Tony had shared with her. Abandoned by his mother, abused by his father, he'd had few positive adult role models in his life.

"Kevin," she said, injecting a calm she didn't feel into her voice. "I want you to sit down."

Frustration and confusion clear in his face, he lifted his fists higher. She tensed, wondering if she'd be fast enough to ward off his blow.

Then, like the cavalry, Tony arrived.

* * *

When Ruby burst into his office yelling about Kevin killing James, Tony took off at a run, knowing Ruby wasn't a drama queen like some of the other girls. But when he hit the kitchen and zigzagged through the obstacle course of Serena, Ari, Brittany and Katy and spotted Kevin looming over Rebecca, Tony nearly lost it.

A cold rage filled him, and for that one instant he could see himself committing the kind of violence his own father had so casually bestowed on his mother. The urge horrified him, but he knew damn well he'd do anything to keep Kevin from harming Rebecca.

"Kevin." Tony leached all emotion from the boy's name. "Back off."

Kevin turned toward him, away from Rebecca. That was good. It would give him a chance to tackle the boy if need be.

Except all the fight seemed to have left Kevin. His hands dropped, his shoulders slumped. Avoiding eye contact with Tony, he turned away and righted the nearest chair. Gaze downcast, he settled his lanky body into it. Head bowed, he closed himself off from the world as he awaited punishment.

Tony hurried to Rebecca's side, only at the last moment resisting the impulse to take her into his arms. Remembering their audience, he put a hand on her shoulder instead. "Are you okay?"

Her voice shook as she answered. "F-fine. He didn't…" She took a breath, and Tony could see the empathy for Kevin in Rebecca's face. "I don't think he would have…"

"He threatened you. That's enough."

She leaned closer, speaking softly. "He's had a rough day. James isn't blameless in this."

"Even still, Kevin stepped over the line." He squeezed her shoulder, giving in to the temptation to draw his fingers down her arm before he let go. He turned to the boys. "Kevin, James. With me, now."

He wouldn't let himself look back at her. He needed one hundred percent focus on the upcoming thunderstorm he was about to deliver on Kevin's head, as well as to come up with some way for these two to bury the hatchet. Another glimpse of Rebecca would just fog his mind.

When they reached his office, Tony directed James to the nearby park bench. Despite the pine tree's shade, the afternoon heat would have him sweating, but maybe the sun would beat some sense into him. Although Kevin was the one who had taken the fight too far, according to Rebecca and Ruby as well, James hadn't been blameless.

Even still, once Tony had Kevin seated in his office, all he could think about was the boy raising his fists to Rebecca. The what-ifs piled up in his mind—what if he'd arrived a few seconds later? What if James had thrown out another taunt? His stomach clenched at the thought.

Kevin hunched in the chair, staring at the floor. Tony remembered being in the boy's shoes, his first few months of foster care before he was placed with Estelle. He'd hated the world and everyone in it.

Estelle had thrown him a lifeline. If he threw one to this mixed up boy, would Kevin even try to catch it?

"Are you ready to leave the program?" Tony asked.

Kevin's head swung up. "I didn't start it. It was James."

"Doesn't matter. What's the rule on fighting?"

"If you kick me out, you should kick him out, too."

"We're talking about you, Kevin."

The boy pushed out his chin in defiance. "It'll take me ten minutes to pack my stuff."

Despite Kevin's insolent tone, Tony could see the fear in his eyes. No foster child had much to pack when they moved from one home to another. But once he had that paper bag filled, where would he go? Tony knew there was nowhere else for Kevin.

Tony might not have given up on the boy, but it seemed Kevin had given up on himself. Tony had to find a way to get through to him. An image of Rebecca flickered in his mind's eye, the kindness in her face, the empathy in her soft brown gaze.

"Any other program, this would be it for you," Tony said, and Kevin's face hardened even further. "But I'm willing to give you another chance."

Joy and relief lit Kevin's face before the boy slid his mask back into place. "Okay."

"I've got a half-dozen chores here on the property that you and James will be taking care of in your spare time. Brush clearing, cleaning drainage ditches, digging post holes for some fencing."

Only a flicker of rebellion lit in Kevin's eyes. "Sure."

"If you mess up again—fight with James, give anyone lip—you will be packing." Tony fixed his gaze on Kevin. "And you'll apologize to Rebecca."

"I will," he said softly. "I'm real sorry."

His dark gaze flicked away from Tony to the floor, to the ceiling, to the walls of the office. Maybe he was searching for courage, because what he finally asked had to have taken a damn lot of bravery. "How do I make Colleen love me again?"

What could he say? When at one time, he himself would have given all the money in the world, his very soul, for that answer where Becca was concerned. When he felt gutted, emptied by Rebecca's abandonment, her clear demonstration that she no longer loved him, he would have done anything to get her back.

Eleven years gone, and the pain had numbed. The part of him that had loved her, had cared so much that she love him back, was dead. Now, despite the clear attraction between them that he couldn't help but acknowledge, Rebecca's love meant little to him emotionally.

Yet he still kept their wedding photo in his file drawer. Tony resolved that after he finished speaking to Kevin and James, he would pull the damn thing from his drawer and throw it in the Dumpster.

He turned his attention back to Kevin. "You can't control who she loves."

Despair and desperation burned in the boy's eyes. "Then how do I stop loving her?"

That he knew the answer to. "You wait. For days, for weeks, for months. Eventually it'll stop hurting."

Kevin nodded, absorbing what Tony had said. "How long did it take you?"

A weight dropped in Tony's stomach. How did Kevin know about his history with Rebecca? It didn't matter, that was forbidden territory as far as he was concerned.

But before he could tell Kevin he'd intruded too far into the personal, the boy added, "When your wife left you and took Lea—did you still love her for a long time?"

The sudden U-turn struck Tony silent for a moment. *Did I ever love her?* The day he and Elena married, he would have sworn he did, that their vows had meant something. But in the ensuing years, as the woman he'd wed changed into a stranger, he began to doubt that love.

Especially when he compared the pallid emotions he'd felt for Elena to the soul-deep devotion he and Rebecca had shared. They'd occupied entirely different universes in his heart.

Kevin still waited for his answer. Tony chose his words with care. "Elena and I were divorced when she left and took Lea away from me. So I'd already...stopped loving her."

In the ensuing quiet, the window AC hummed, its gust of coolness impotent against the summer heat. Inexplicably, the chilled air against his face reminded him of Rebecca, of the long, hot August nights of their eighteen months of marriage. She would keep a wet hand towel in the refrigerator and stroke it against his skin as they lay in bed together. He hadn't thought of those times in years, but the images rolled over him, as fresh as if they'd happened yesterday.

He resolutely shut the door on the past. "Send James in here on your way out."

In the moments between Kevin's departure and James's arrival, when he should have been formulating what he'd say to the second boy, he let the memories in again. Rebecca's soft voice, whispering in the dark, her hand drawing the cold towel over his back, drawing the heat of the day from his body. Her rounded belly brushing against him as she stretched out beside him. The feel of the baby moving against his hand.

A fist closed tight around his heart, blotting out the sunlight, the warm day, the AC's hum. James had to all but shout his name to pull him from the darkness.

Ignoring the puzzled look on the boy's face, Tony ordered him to sit, then read him the riot act.

Chapter Seven

Kevin came straight to Rebecca after leaving Tony's office and gave her the most heartfelt apology she'd ever heard. Tall and slender where Tony had been shorter and stockier, nevertheless the boy's dark hair and eyes brought back memories of Tony at nineteen. The same serious face, the same banked fire hidden behind a protective shield he held up to the world.

With the white sauce scorched and the weather too hot for anything heavy, Rebecca switched gears and talked her crew through a chicken Caesar salad. While Kevin and Brittany grilled the chicken, James and Katy prepared the dressing and Ruby and Colleen tore romaine into chunks. Serena and Ari cubed day-old sourdough they'd picked up from the farmer's market, drizzled the pieces with olive oil and garlic, then baked them into croutons.

By the time they gathered around the table, color had blossomed in James's left eye and cheek where Kevin's fist had made contact. His knuckles raw, Kevin winced when Ari's hand brushed his as she passed the bread basket. He didn't offer up so much as a word of complaint.

As if they were all shell-shocked by James and Kevin's confrontation, the teens were quiet and subdued as they ate. Serena said please and thank-you when she asked Colleen to pass the bread and butter, James asked if anyone else wanted more fresh strawberries before he took the last glistening red fruit.

Seated beside Rebecca, Estelle looked on with a bemused smile on her face. "Nothing like the fear of God to put someone on the straight and narrow."

"Fear of Tony, you mean," Rebecca said. Estelle had filled her in on Tony's ultimatum. James and Kevin both knew they were living on borrowed time if they stepped so much as a toe over the line.

"He really cares about these kids." Estelle pushed her salad around on her plate. "He wants desperately for them to succeed."

Rebecca lowered her voice. "Then why isn't he here? Why does he hole up in the house and wait for Jana to bring him his meals?"

Estelle speared a morsel of grilled chicken. "I think you know why."

"However he feels about me," Rebecca said softly, "he has to put it aside for these kids."

Estelle shrugged, rearranging the crisp chunks of romaine into a pile. For the first time, Rebecca realized the older woman had barely eaten a bite.

"Why aren't you eating?"

Estelle gestured with her fork. "I guess I snacked too much during dinner prep."

Except Estelle hadn't shown up until it was time to serve. Worry nibbled at Rebecca. But when she would have pursued the issue, Estelle called out, "Anyone want to go into town for a movie?"

A clamor rose around the table, excited discussion of which films were playing and who wanted to see what. Beside her, Lea tugged on her arm. "Can I go?"

"We'd have to ask your daddy." Rebecca glanced over at Estelle, saw the way her shoulders sagged with tiredness. "I'll go talk to him."

"He's in his office," Jana told her. "Catching up on paperwork."

With the sun barely touching the tops of the pines, the air still sizzled with heat as Rebecca stepped outside. She had to force herself to slow her pace, to resist running headlong toward Tony's office. She wanted to see him far too much.

She paused in the shade of the black oak, sinking onto the bench beneath it. She seemed to spend so many moments of her day in anticipation of when she'd next see Tony. Those few miserly minutes she saw him each evening were never enough.

It must be the heat and the drama of the teens' lives that had her so off balance. Spending so much time with these eighteen- and nineteen-year-old girls and boys had her reliving the tumult of her own past. Why would she want to revisit the pain of that time?

Reeling in her emotions, she crossed the thick carpet of pine needles to Tony's door. A brisk knock to announce her presence, then she slipped inside.

He looked up at her, startled. Papers scattered across his

KAREN SANDLER   89

desk, he held something in his hand—a framed picture? She could swear color rose in his cheeks as he turned the picture facedown on his desk.

"Having another problem with James and Kevin?" he asked.

She pulled over a chair for herself. "Estelle suggested an outing to the movies. Lea wants to go."

He scraped his fingers through his hair. "I can't go with her. Too much to do here."

"Between us, we can keep an eye on her." She glanced at the frame under his hand. "Is that a photo of Lea?"

"What? No." He stuffed the picture into a desk drawer. "Anything else?"

Talk to me. Tell me what's going between us. Help me make sense of this craziness I'm feeling.

But she couldn't say that out loud. "I'm a little worried about Estelle. She seems tired, under the weather. Her back has really been hurting."

"I've offered to take her to the doctor more than once. She says she's fine."

"Do you think she'd tell us if she wasn't?"

He shook his head. "I'll keep after her. What about the kids—will they clean up their act? We only have four weeks until opening."

Rebecca considered what she'd been rolling around in her mind since her conversation with Estelle. "They need you, Tony. They do what I ask them to do, but you're the one they see as the final authority. You're the father none of them had."

"They can come to me anytime they want."

"You need to go to them." Rebecca took a breath. "When I asked you to let me be in charge of the kitchen,

I didn't mean you should stay away. You need to sit down with them. Break bread. Share a meal. Listen to them vent."

His jaw tightened, but he nodded. "I'll be there in the morning for breakfast. Anything else?"

Nothing she was willing to speak out loud. She pushed from her chair. "I'll see you tomorrow, then."

Feeling his gaze on her, she left his office. At the bakeshop, the teens had finished their cleanup in record time. They'd settled on a kid-friendly movie, but even with Kevin bowing out, there weren't enough seats in Jana's and Rebecca's cars for everyone.

Just as well; Rebecca had lost interest in seeing a film. "Ruby can drive my car," she told the others. "I've got laundry to finish."

Tears filled Lea's eyes. "Don't wanna go without you."

Jana picked up the little girl and gave her a hug. "Hey, sweetpea, Grams and I would be pretty sad if we left you behind."

Estelle brushed a tear from Lea's cheek. "You can hold my hand the whole time during the movie, honey. I'd sure like you to come."

A worry line creasing her forehead, Lea turned to Rebecca. "Will you be here when I get back?"

Lea's soft query knocked the air from Rebecca's lungs. "Of course, sweetheart. And besides," she leaned in even closer to whisper, "how could I leave? You'll have my car."

Lea flashed a brief smile at the reminder. "Will you read to me tomorrow night?"

"Just like always. As many stories as you like."

Her fears allayed, Lea climbed into the backseat of

Rebecca's Corolla beside Estelle. With Keystone Cops hilarity, the rest of the crowd squeezed into the two cars and headed off to Placerville.

By the time Rebecca made a last pass through the kitchen and dining room, it was a quarter after eight. As she locked up, the sun had finally set behind the trees and the air had cooled to a bearable temperature. To the west, bands of coral and red still striped the sky, to the east, blackness had seeped into the treetops.

Rebecca felt restless and edgy as she returned to the empty guest cottage. With Lea gone, she didn't even have a bedtime story to look forward to. She had laundry to fold once she retrieved it from the dryer and a new recipe book to look over. After that, she was at loose ends.

Tony's office was dark; no doubt he'd gone into the house. Knowing he was there, alone, so close, only added to her agitation. The exact thing she longed to do—go to him—was the last thing she ought to do.

Grabbing her basket, she headed for the laundry room that was built onto the far end of the bunkhouse. Through the open windows of the bunkhouse, she saw Kevin on the sofa, a book in his lap. He spotted her walking by and nodded in acknowledgment.

Her one small chore was completed much too quickly. Unwilling to sit and peruse the recipe book, she headed outside again and walked along the path that led toward the back of the main house. Intrigued by the pergola over-grown with wisteria in the back corner of Tony's yard, she made her way toward it.

Without a moon, with only the light from the house il-luminating the yard, she had to strain to see the opening in the curtain of twisted vines. When she stepped within the thick leafy growth, she saw the bench inside it. Then she saw Tony.

She stopped, began to retreat. "I'm sorry. I didn't know you were here."

His voice floated out from the darkness. "Sit with me, Rebecca."

The closeness of the densely covered pergola seemed far too intimate. But her longing for Tony, for his company, for his nearness, flooded Rebecca. The incomprehensible ache she'd felt inside all week filled her.

Moving carefully in the dark, she sat beside him on the stone bench. The tangle of wisteria vines stood out in silhouette against the lights from the house. It was as if they were in a living cave, hidden from the world. She shut her eyes, feeling the sweet summer air, full of mysteries, stroke her cheek.

Tony rested his hand on the bench between them. "Estelle had wisteria climbing her back porch. Do you remember?"

With his arm so close to hers, she could feel the warmth of his skin. She ought to pull away, but instead she leaned closer. "I just remember there was that little corner in the back where no one could see us. We would pretend someone cast a spell on us and made us invisible."

They'd been young and innocent that year she lived at Estelle's, their imaginations filled with fairies and wizards. Later, when she was back with her parents, she spent three afternoons a week at the foster home while her mother worked. Then there were those occasional Saturday nights her parents would let her sleep over. She and Tony would spin stories into the wee hours.

She wished she could bring back that childhood innocence, forget the darkness that fell over them. Wash away the tears they'd shed.

"The night I kissed you," Tony said, his voice rumbling in her ear, "I felt bewitched."

He couldn't have been more than a millimeter from her, so close the slightest shift would bring them into contact. The images flashed in quick succession—the two of them on Estelle's porch. She was eighteen, Tony twenty. She could still see him dipping his head down, feel the first gentle contact of his mouth.

Elation had rocketed through her. She'd been feeling more for him than friendship for months, and when he'd suggested they go together to Estelle's to visit their former foster mother, she'd gladly agreed. That night during dinner, and afterward as they caught up in Estelle's kitchen, every glance from him set off explosions inside her. She'd wondered what those heated looks meant. The instant he kissed her, she knew.

She felt breathless remembering. "I never wanted you to stop."

He drew his fingers along her arm, from bare wrist to the sleeve of her knit top. "I would have kissed you all night if Estelle hadn't come looking for us."

A part of her wished Estelle was here right now, to tell them to quit this nonsense and go home. But she was an adult, didn't need her foster mother to tell her she was blundering into dangerous territory.

She knew that all on her own. "We were too young," she said, as if that would stop the sensations shivering along her skin.

His breath curled against her cheek. "We knew what we wanted."

What they wanted still. She didn't resist when his hands cradled her face, turned her mouth up to his. She parted her lips with a sigh with his first touch, welcomed his tongue inside. Her hands spread across his chest, reveled in the heat, the strength there.

His groan vibrated through her body, sparked along her nerve endings. He pulled her closer, his arms enfolding her in warmth. His mouth never leaving hers, he lifted her from the bench into his lap. Against her hip, she felt the hard length of him. She thought her heart would explode from her chest.

"I wanted you so much that night," he rasped out. "I would have taken you on the back porch."

"I would have let you."

As he tugged up her shirt, bared her to the night air, memories of the past entwined with the present, like the wisteria vines woven into the pergola. His large hand spanned her waist, trailed a path upward, settling just under her breast. Her bra felt restrictive, too tight, and she wanted desperately to unhook it and slip it off.

"It was only a month until we finally slept together," he murmured. "But it seemed like forever."

His mouth moved along her jaw, feathering kisses that warmed her skin, set off an ache low in her body. His hand drew lazy circles on her rib cage, his thumb brushing the bottom of her breast, teasing her through the thin knit of her bra. When he grazed her nipple, the breath left her lungs, and she thought she would melt in his arms.

A month after that night at Estelle's, her parents were out of town and he'd come to her house. They'd made love in her room, in a twin bed barely wide enough for the two of them. Three weeks later she was staring at a little blue stripe on a home pregnancy test stick.

What if it had happened at Estelle's instead, a month earlier? Would the pregnancy have been different, stronger somehow? Maybe a different doctor would have been in the emergency room, someone who could have worked a miracle, who could have saved their baby.

"Oh, God," Rebecca gasped, pulling away from Tony. Shaking all over, she stumbled to her feet. "I can't do this."

She could see the faint gleam of his eyes. "Why not?" Before she could formulate an answer, he stood. "Never mind. I'm a damned idiot."

She turned away, wanting nothing more than to be alone in her room. To stuff away in the Pandora's box inside her all the imps and demons that kept trying to escape.

"Wait," he said. "I'll walk with you."

She'd just as soon he leave her be, but didn't have the energy for an argument. They followed the path to the cottage in silence.

Opening the door, she forced herself to lift her gaze to his. In the glow of the porch light, he looked so weary, it was all she could do to keep from throwing her arms around him again.

Then he turned and walked away. As she watched those broad shoulders receding in the dark, her heart ached. It took all her will to hold back the tears until she'd reached the privacy of her room.

Chapter Eight

The heat wave broke, temperatures plunging fifteen degrees almost overnight. While the cooling trend helped soothe the teens' volatile tempers, it was Tony's presence at nearly every meal that kept everyone on an even keel.

Everyone except Rebecca. She spent her days in constant anticipation of seeing him again. When she should have been concentrating on teaching the students how to braid a loaf of challah or how to keep a hollandaise from curdling, Tony was always at the periphery of her consciousness.

The first week, when Tony would show up just as the meal was being served and leave immediately after they'd finished, she'd managed to cope. Knowing when to expect him, how long he'd stay made it easier to keep her rampant emotions in check. He'd keep his distance from her, maintaining his focus on the kids.

But the second week, he started arriving a few minutes early for dinner to help ferry the food from kitchen to dining room. Then he turned up even earlier each evening to assist the teens with table setup. By the end of the third week, he was reporting to the kitchen at the start of dinner prep, taking a place for himself in the work crew. He still maintained an invisible barrier between himself and Rebecca, but she felt the connection sizzling between them nevertheless.

Now, as Rebecca schooled Brittany and Ruby in the preparation of orange spiced walnuts to be used as a salad topper, Tony and Katy worked together on pricing the evening's meal. Although they wouldn't be serving falafel pita sandwiches and spanakopitas when the bakeshop opened, Ari's suggestion for Friday night's meal fit well with Rebecca's desire that her students master a wide and varied cuisine repertoire. She also insisted they keep up the exercise of calculating food costs for everything they prepared.

"Keep the walnuts moving in the pan so they don't scorch," she told Ruby as she turned away from the stove.

Her gaze strayed to Tony across the kitchen. He and Katy were seated at a length of counter they'd designated "the office." As Tony supervised, Katy worked a calculator with one hand while her pencil in the other scribbled on a pad of paper.

As if he sensed her watching him, Tony turned. His dark gaze locked with hers, knotting the tantalizing thread of awareness between them.

Seeing his attention had strayed, Katy looked over her shoulder at Rebecca. "When do I get to use the laptop like the others?"

Rebecca had allowed everyone but Katy use of her

laptop computer to do the meal pricing. "When Tony tells me you completely understand the process by hand."

Katy released a heavy sigh and returned to her labors. Tony's gaze lingered on Rebecca a few moments longer, sending her messages she told herself she had no business intercepting.

Turning her back on him, she directed her attention to James and Kevin working at the deep fryer. They were scooping out balls of mashed chickpeas, onions and spices and dropping them in the deep-fryer basket. A couple dozen falafels were keeping warm in the oven, spread out on a paper towel–lined cookie sheet. On the center island, Ari was cutting in half the homemade pitas she'd baked after lunch. Colleen was getting a head start on cleanup while Serena set the table.

Jana entered the kitchen with Lea. "Grams says she isn't hungry. She said to bring a plate over to the bunk-house for later."

Tony's gaze met Rebecca's again. The worry she felt for Estelle was mirrored in his eyes. He slipped off the kitchen stool. "I'll take care of it."

He stuffed a pita half with three falafels, added lettuce and tomato, then drizzled in some tahini. Ruby had just tossed the salad with the walnuts, and she served a portion beside the pita sandwich. Brittany unearthed a brownie from one of the freezers and handed that over.

While Ruby covered the plate, Tony cornered Rebecca by the freezer. "Do you have a few minutes after dinner?"

Nothing in his face gave her a clue to the reason for his request. "Sure," she told him.

With his back to the others, he shielded her from their view. "Something I need to talk to you about."

He glanced over his shoulder at the busy teens, then back at her. "Rebecca…" He lifted his hand to her face, stroked her cheek so lightly she could barely feel the contact.

But it was enough to send sensation through her from head to toe. Those moments in the pergola, their kisses in the dark, flashed through her mind's eye.

Ruby's voice jarred them apart. "The plate's ready for Grams."

Tony turned away from her, swept up Estelle's dinner and strode from the kitchen.

By the time Tony returned from the bunkhouse, the others were all seated at the dinner table. The only empty spot was next to Rebecca. A mixed blessing—he wanted nothing more than to be near her but didn't trust his self-control. Considering the way he'd touched her in the kitchen with everyone present, he wasn't entirely certain he wouldn't do something just as stupid here in the dining room.

Since that night in the pergola, he felt as if he struggled for balance on a razor edge. On one side, the same tight discipline he'd demanded of himself for years, on the other, the complete surrender to the magnetic pull that was Rebecca. Every moment spent in her domain, here in the bakeshop, he was certain he would go ballistic if he didn't touch her, press his mouth against hers.

Forbidden fruit, that was all it was. If he could talk to her, demystify the intense attraction, maybe it would ease enough to save his sanity. An awkward discussion, but if he did nothing, he might be giving these teens an explicit lesson he'd just as soon not teach them.

Serving himself a falafel sandwich and salad, he brought his plate to the table. As he sat, Rebecca glanced at him, a query in her eyes. It was clear she wanted to know what was going on with Estelle. He wasn't about to keep what he knew from her, but for the moment would just as soon keep the rest of them in the dark. Which meant he'd have to lean close so he could speak softly into her ear.

Which also meant confronting the temptation to brush his lips against her hair, kiss the whorls of her ear. He blocked the impulse from his mind. "She told me she was tired and wanted to eat alone."

Rebecca leaned in just as close to murmur, "Do you believe that?"

He suppressed the shudder that traveled down his spine. "She's not well." He kept his voice barely above a whisper. "I told her if she didn't make an appointment with her doctor, I would."

"Good." She lifted her gaze to his, her chocolate-brown eyes stealing his breath. "Thank you."

He picked up his sandwich, determined to direct his mind toward something other than Rebecca's fragrance, the warmth of her skin. Across the table, Lea was focused on her disintegrating pita, tahini sauce decorating her face from ear to ear.

"Has she been sleeping any better?" Rebecca asked softly.

"Two nightmares this week, one Sunday, one last night." He'd sat up in bed with her all night, catnapping with the little girl's tense body in his arms. "I thought we were done with the bad dreams."

"She's still processing what happened."

He knew that, had shepherded enough young people

through the aftermath of traumatic life events when he worked as a school counselor. But when it was his own daughter struggling with the fear and grief, it was harder to be clearheaded.

As he brooded over Lea's recent setback, the teens chattered, their conversation flying around the table at light speed. James told a goofy joke that made Lea laugh; Ruby shared the plot of the book assigned by her online college class.

With a grant from one of the local tech companies, Tony had been able to set up two bleeding-edge computers in the bunkhouse for the teens' use. While computer games were the main attraction for most of the kids, Ruby used the system for her only class. He was gratified that both Serena and Ari had expressed interest in registering for similar classes in the fall.

He didn't touch Rebecca, didn't lean in close again to whisper in her ear. But her thigh was only inches from his under the table, her arm so close to his where it rested beside her plate, he could swear he felt her heat. It would take only a careless move of his hand to brush against hers, to feel the silky texture of her skin.

He barely tasted his food, scarcely comprehended the flow of conversation around him. It wasn't until she rose and took his plate and hers to the kitchen that the pounding of his heart eased. He could finally put two thoughts together and return his focus to the teens.

But as difficult as it was being within touching distance of her, he knew she'd been right—the kids needed him here. James and Kevin's interactions still needed a few sharp edges polished. Rather than separate the boys, he turned them into a team, tasking them to folding and stowing the tables before mopping the floor. When the girls' argument over who would scrape, who would load the dishwasher, who would put away the dishes escalated into high drama, he stepped in. Everyone counted to ten, then levelheaded Ruby got the work parceled out to everyone's satisfaction.

Throughout the cleanup, his gaze strayed again and again to Rebecca. As she threaded herself amongst the disparate teens, keeping them woven together into a cohesive group, her every movement fascinated him. The way she kept Lea in the mix, giving his daughter easy jobs to complete like stuffing the napkin holders or bringing salt and pepper shakers into the kitchen, sent a warmth through him that alarmed and confused him.

Then the teens drifted off to the bunkhouse, all of them keen to say good-night to Estelle. Jana hesitated at the door, stifling a yawn. "I'll take Lea up to the main house if you like. I'm not meeting Ian until eight."

"Thanks," Tony said. "I'd appreciate that."

Then it was just him and Rebecca. He took up a post at the door, crossing his arms over his chest to keep himself from reaching for her. She was like a perpetual motion machine, moving through the kitchen to tweak a fragment of food from the deep fryer, giving the stainless steel counters one last swipe with a paper towel. Eventually she'd have to stop, eventually she'd have to come over to the door, to leave if nothing else.

Open your mouth, he told himself. *Lay it out for her.* Then they could go their separate ways and he could get his head on straight again. But he couldn't seem to break the silence, too entranced by her every move.

Finally, she turned to him, the island between them. "What was it you wanted?"

He took the coward's way out, opening the conversation with the mundane. "Sam Harrison will be here on opening day. He said he's looking forward to seeing how the program is going."

Sam was the main benefactor of Estelle's House, but thus far hadn't shown much interest in the day-to-day ins and outs of the independent-living program Tony had created. But Sam was excited about attending the opening, which gratified Tony.

Rebecca spread her hands on the island's butcher-block top. "I'm surprised we haven't seen him before now."

"He told me he's been swamped with deadlines and book tours." Tony's longtime friend was a bestselling thriller novelist; three of his books had been adapted into blockbuster movies.

"It'll be nice to see him again. I haven't seen him since…"

He could see that particular memory bubbling up in her mind as clearly as if she'd finished her sentence. The last time she'd seen Sam was the night he'd driven her to the airport down in Sacramento. It had taken Tony an angry ten months to forgive his friend for facilitating Rebecca's departure.

"If you'd told me that night you wanted to leave," he managed to say, "I would have taken you."

Her frank disbelief was obvious. "You never would have let me go. We would have spent another six months hurting each other until I could get up the courage again."

Then why leave at all? He'd never completely understood it, never come close to forgiving it. Intellectually, he comprehended that she was hurting; they both were. But why couldn't they have worked it through together?

That was a question he'd asked himself a thousand times in the last eleven years. It was pointless to ask it now.

"I have work to do." She moved toward the door, no doubt expecting him to step aside.

If he wasn't going to come clean, then he ought to get out of her way. But having her so tantalizingly close during dinner tonight, during all their shared meals over the last several weeks had messed with his brain. When it should have been telling his feet to move, instead he stood planted. Even worse, his hand swept off the light. With the sun just settling behind the trees, sunset painted the kitchen's white walls with coral. Brushed her cheeks with the same soft palette.

"You're right," he told her. "If it had been up to me, I never would have let you go."

"But there wasn't anything left of our marriage by then."

Nothing but the bald truth, but it still had the power to wound him. All that time ago, it should have been ancient history. There shouldn't be anything left in him to care anymore.

He gulped in a breath. "About what's going on between you and me."

She lifted a wary brow. "Yes?"

Now why did even that one word sound like an invitation? Damn, he had it bad. "I want to lay it on the table." He shoved his hands into his pockets to keep from touching her. "I still want you. As much as—no, more than—I ever did when we were young and stupid."

He looked away, feeling heat rise in his cheeks, then back at her. "If not for these kids, my daughter… If not for our history…I'd have you in my bed."

Her eyes widened, the pupils in the dimming room growing larger. As they did when they'd made love.

He banished that memory. "That doesn't mean there's anything else between us. What we had during our marriage…we both know that's dead. If my kissing you led you to believe it meant anything beyond physical attraction, if you thought I wanted something more—"

"Of course not." The steel in her chocolate brown eyes gave way to softness. "I know what we had before is gone. That we can't go back."

He should feel satisfied that she understood, that they were in agreement. But somehow, nothing felt settled.

She edged toward the door again, and this time he moved out of her way. He gave Rebecca her space while she locked the door, walking alongside her until the path split toward the main house.

When he reached the house, he got a reprieve. Lea was so exhausted by the previous night's ordeal she'd fallen asleep on the sofa while she and Jana waited for Tony.

He carefully picked Lea up to carry her to bed. "Before you leave for your date, can you tell Rebecca no story time for tonight?"

"Sure." Jana made a face. "Ian flaked on me. I'm not meeting him after all."

She headed out while Tony started up the stairs. Lea was well and truly in dreamland, not stirring at all when he set her on the bed and slipped off her sandals. It was still too warm for the covers, so he just pulled the sheet over her. With faint sunlight filtering through the window, the room wasn't dark yet, but would be within the hour. He flipped on the night-light just in case Lea woke.

He lingered in the doorway and watched over his daughter. If only he could reach inside her mind and wipe away the old and ugly memories that brought the night-

mares. He didn't want her to forget her mother—he knew
Elena had loved Lea in her own way—but no four-year-
old should have to harbor the kind of terror, anguish and
grief that his daughter did.

What if he could do the same for himself? Forget
forever the love he'd once felt for Rebecca. Obliterate the
agony of losing his firstborn on that horrific night twelve
years ago, then the anguish when Becca left a year later.
Would he be willing to sacrifice the months of joy as he
and Rebecca anticipated the birth of their child to save
himself the torment of his death?

His throat constricted at the thought. He couldn't erase
his son from existence, stillborn or not. That baby boy had
been vital and alive for eight months. A part of him was
still lodged deep in Tony's heart.

Alejandro. His last, his only gift to his son had been a
name. Something to be buried with, carved into a grave
marker.

The tightness in his throat sharpened, sorrow pricking
his eyes with tears. He crossed the room, leaning over to
press a gentle kiss on his daughter's forehead. Inside, he
wailed for the brother this little girl would never know.

After her unsettling confrontation with Tony, disappointment and relief had equal footing inside Rebecca
when Jana returned to tell her Lea had fallen asleep. Even
with the expectation that she wouldn't have seen Tony
anyway during story time, she would still be hyperaware
of him just on the other side of his daughter's bedroom
wall.

She didn't even have the solitude she'd been anticipat-
ing tonight with Jana's date cancelled. She generally

enjoyed the younger girl's company, but tonight she just wanted to hide from the turmoil running laps in her stomach. She could have holed up in her bedroom, but it was barely eight-thirty. She'd go stir-crazy in that small room for the three or so hours until bedtime.

Jana was easy enough to ignore, sprawled on the sofa and zoned out on a reality show. She didn't even notice Rebecca crossing in front of the TV to access the laptop and printer she'd set up in the living room.

In preparation for a Saturday morning meeting in lieu of their customary farmer's market visit, Rebecca had typed up and printed out lists of everything the students had prepared thus far in the five weeks she'd been here. Tomorrow they'd go over the list and finalize the bake-shop's menu. They'd already decided on a half-dozen standards—buttermilk coffee cake, apple turnovers, peach cobbler, apple fritters, hot spiced apple cider and caramel-topped poached pears. She wanted to add in two or three specials that they'd cycle through on a weekly basis.

The lists collated and spread out on the dinette table, she went back to her bedroom for her stapler. It was missing from the top of her postage stamp–sized desk. A search of the drawers also came up empty.

"Jana, have you seen my stapler?" she called out the door of her room.

"Sorry." Muting the television, Jana popped up from the couch. "I couldn't find Tony's and borrowed yours. It's in his office."

Rebecca squelched her irritation. "Can I borrow your key?" Tony hadn't given her a key to the office since she had no need for one.

"Sure." As she dug in her pocket, her cell phone rang.

Jana dove for it, snatching it from the coffee table. A smile lit her face. "Hey, babe."

Ian, no doubt, and her boyfriend's call had apparently sidetracked Jana from giving Rebecca the key. When she stepped into the girl's line of sight as a reminder, Jana rose, grabbed her purse from the floor beside the sofa and motioned Rebecca toward the door.

As they stepped outside, she said goodbye and snapped shut her phone. "I'm going over to his place. He didn't have to go in to work after all. I'll let you in on my way out."

At Tony's office, Jana unlocked the door, then flipped on the light switch. Rebecca stepped past her into the cluttered office. "Where did you leave it?" she asked when a quick scan didn't reveal the stapler.

"On the desk." Jana followed her inside. "Maybe Tony put it in his desk." She reached for the top left drawer.

"I don't feel comfortable going through his things."

"He doesn't keep anything in here but office stuff." She tried the right hand drawer. No luck. "He's sent me in here to get things for him. I'm sure he won't mind."

She yanked open the middle drawer. A familiar object lay facedown inside. The picture frame Tony had been holding a few weeks ago when she'd come to speak with him. Jana pulled it out to see better inside the drawer. Laid it faceup on the desk.

Shock jolted through Rebecca as she registered the image in the tarnished silver frame. Too stunned for a moment to snatch it up and hide it again, she lost her opportunity as Jana came up empty-handed from her search and her gaze fell on the photo.

Their wedding picture. Tony and Becca Herrera, so

very much in love, with all the joy of the day written in their smiling faces.

"Holy…" Jana's voice faded as she picked up the framed photo. "This is you and…" She looked from the picture to Rebecca. "You were married."

Chapter Nine

As Rebecca braced herself for a barrage of questions, Jana's cell rang. Ian again, this time asking her to pick up a six-pack on her way to his place. Grateful for the interruption, Rebecca returned the wedding photo to the desk drawer, facedown as before, hopefully in about the same spot. While Jana wriggled with impatience, Rebecca scanned the office for her stapler, finally spotting it behind a ream of paper on the filing cabinet.

Jana hustled her out of the office and made a dash for her car. "See you in the morning."

It wouldn't be the first time the girl had stayed over at Ian's. Since she had the weekend off, Jana might not be back until Sunday. That would forestall for a couple days Jana spreading the word to the others of what she'd discovered. Rebecca wasn't sure the girl could be counted on to keep quiet, even if asked.

As she made her way back to the guest cottage, Rebecca's whirling thoughts returned again and again to the same realization. Tony had kept their wedding picture. He'd held on to it all these years, kept it not stowed away in a box somewhere but in his desk drawer where he might come across it on a daily basis.

They'd only had the one photo, taken by Darius Jones, Tony's P.I. friend who had found Lea. Estelle had given them the frame as a wedding gift. Rebecca had always intended to scan the photo and get some wallet-sized copies made so they could each have one, but either money or time had been tight and she'd never gotten around to it. Then the baby died and it hadn't mattered anymore. Carrying that picture in her purse would have just cut more deeply into her heart.

So why had Tony kept it? After all that talk earlier about the past being dead and gone, why would he save the only memento of their short marriage?

Back at the cottage, she quickly finished her simple task of stapling the stacks of paper. With Friday night stretching out endlessly before her, she curled up on the sofa with a book. After reading the same paragraph three times without making sense of it, she switched on the television. Ten restless minutes of channel flipping later, she turned the TV off and dropped the remote on the sofa.

Eyes shut, she tried to still her mind. But somehow, all she could think of was Tony and the ebulliently happy faces in that photo.

If he hadn't come downstairs for a glass of water, he would have missed the faint tapping on the front door. His first thought was Estelle, that maybe she'd taken a turn for the worse and one of the teens had come to fetch him. He would have thought they'd call, but maybe they didn't want to risk waking Lea.

He wasn't at all prepared to see Rebecca standing under the front-porch light. "Can I come in?" she asked.

He considered. Would it be better to stay outside? Away from that inviting sofa, the room lit only by a small table lamp beside it? But the porch had its own perils, bringing back memories of Estelle's Sacramento home, the long nights spent in intimate conversation.

In any case, he had to be able to listen for Lea. He stepped aside, holding the screen door for Rebecca. The moment she'd crossed the threshold, he turned on every light in the living room until it was daytime bright.

At his gestured invitation, she perched on the edge of the easy chair at right angles to the sofa. He sat on the sofa, keeping some distance between them.

She glanced upstairs. "So she went down easily tonight?"

"Fell asleep with her head in Jana's lap."

"Do you think she'll sleep through?"

He shrugged. "I'm trying not to get my hopes up too much."

Her gaze dropped to her laced fingers in her lap. "I needed my stapler tonight. Jana told me she'd left it in your office. While we were looking for it, we opened your desk drawer."

The picture. "She saw it?" Rebecca nodded in response to his question. "What did you tell her?"

"Not much. Two minutes later she was off to Ian's place."

"Then there's still time to talk to her." He reached for the portable phone, beside him on a side table. "Tell her to keep it to herself."

As he dialed, he heard a noise from Lea's room. Not a scream, yet. Just a whimper. About to drop the phone, he was forestalled by Rebecca. "I'll check on her."

Jana's cell went to voice mail. He left a brief message asking her to call him. Then he hurried upstairs.

He hesitated in the doorway, taking in the scene before him. Rebecca sat on the edge of Lea's bed, stroking his daughter's back, humming softly. He remembered the lullaby—she'd sung it for their unborn child, caressing her pregnant belly the same way she did Lea. She'd wanted the baby to come to know her voice. To know who his mother was the moment he was born.

She sang the song on the way to the E.R., her voice choked with tears, blood soaking the towel they'd spread under her. Crooning to a child who likely was already dead, no longer listening to his mother's lullaby.

Rebecca turned to look over her shoulder at him and he could see the sheen of tears in her eyes. The same memories must be crowding her mind, pounding on her heart. The knife had to be cutting her even more sharply than him, and he was in agony remembering.

His daughter quiet now, he held out his hand to Rebecca. As she clutched his fingers, he led her from the room, along the landing, down the stairs. Although tears spilled down her cheeks, she swallowed back her grief until they'd returned to the living-room sofa.

He held her in his arms as she sobbed, loud and ugly. Her fingernails dug into his shoulders as she gripped him, her body shaking so hard he feared she would hurt herself.

His face was wet, too, the images of that small, still body burned into his mind. The twelve years since he died should have dulled the pain. Why couldn't they let it go?

Finally, she fell into silence, releasing him as she pulled away. Her hands trembled as she tried to wipe her cheeks dry.

"I'll be right back," he told her as he got to his feet. He went to the downstairs bathroom for a box of tissues and to fill a paper cup with water. When he returned, he pulled several tissues from the box and gave them to her, then swiped one across his own face.

Her eyes were still red even after she'd blotted up the tears. She gulped the water he offered, then set the cup aside. Hugging herself, she lifted her gaze to him.

"Do you go to his grave?" she asked.

A lump lodged in his throat. "On Easter Sunday. El Dia del Muerte. His birthday." Alejandro had been born November 28.

"I went so often the year after he died. But I haven't been to see him since I left eleven years ago." Tears threatened again. "What kind of mother does that make me?"

"You can't beat yourself up about the past, Rebecca."

"Why not? You do." She wiped away her tears with an impatient hand. "What difference does it make if they know we were married? We were in love, we made a baby together. Are you ashamed of that?"

Of course he wasn't. He just didn't want to complicate things by revealing the personal connection between him and Rebecca. "You're right. There's no need to keep it secret."

Legs folded under her, she settled back into the corner of the sofa. He should have anticipated what she said next, but it caught him unprepared. "You kept the picture."

"I meant to throw it away. Tried to a hundred times."

Pain flickered in her eyes. "We were so happy that day. I wish…"

"What?"

"Sometimes I wish I'd known. Before we got married. That the baby…" She hitched in a breath. "That Alejandro wasn't going to…" Her eyes squeezed shut. "Damn it."

Silence ticked away as Rebecca seemed to struggle for control. "I can't wait for his birthday. Will you go with me on Sunday?"

As vulnerable as he'd been with her tonight, he'd be ten times more exposed at the cemetery. That small rectangle of black stone had the power to bring him to his knees.

But how could he refuse? When those soft brown eyes pleaded with him, there was only one possible answer he could give her.

"Estelle will watch Lea. I'll go to early mass and take you after."

Rather than wait for Tony, Rebecca suggested she join him at the eight o'clock mass at St. Patrick's in Placerville. So they left the ranch together at a quarter after seven, stopping at the supermarket in town for a bouquet of flowers and a small teddy bear. Rebecca had brought a plastic vase, and they put the vibrant gladiolas and irises in it to keep them fresh. She held the teddy bear in her lap and the vase between her feet, the real flowers a riotous display against the more muted floral pattern of her skirt.

When she stepped inside the church, she felt a twinge of guilt at how long it had been since she'd attended any service. Her faith, never strong, had been tattered when her parents were so badly hurt; Alejandro's death had shattered her willingness to believe. Over the years, she'd rebuilt a tenuous relationship with God, finding it a buttress to her lonely life.

Tony's devotion to his church had always surprised her, considering the hell his life had been with his father. Although she hadn't been raised a Catholic, she'd often attended services with Tony during that year at Estelle's. During their marriage, despite their civil ceremony, Sunday morning mass became a tradition, often followed by breakfast with Estelle.

They'd been making plans to baptize the baby only a month before they lost him. Instead of celebrating that joyful occasion, Tony's parish priest performed last rites at the hospital.

As they stepped from the church into the late August sunshine after services were over, Rebecca wondered if Tony was thinking about when their world had fallen apart. She wouldn't allow herself to bring the memories into sharp focus, couldn't bear recalling the agony of that black night. But sitting in the mass with Tony, gazing up at the tall stained-glass windows behind the altar, she felt inundated by the past.

They stopped in town for breakfast, although the moment the waitress set the scrambled eggs and toast she'd ordered in front of her, her stomach clenched. Knowing she had to at least make an effort, she spread strawberry jam on a toast triangle. "Did Jana ever call you back?"

Tony picked at his Denver omelet. "We've been playing phone tag."

She nibbled her toast without enthusiasm. "Considering the looks I was getting from Serena and Ari during the meeting yesterday, I think the cat is out of the bag. Jana's got the whole group on speed dial."

He shrugged. "We'll talk to them tonight."

"And if they ask why we split up?"

He stared across the table at her. "You left me, Rebecca," he said softly. "What am I supposed to say?"

Tears stung her eyes. "There was more to it than that, Tony. We weren't…I couldn't…"

He sighed. "We'll just tell them things didn't work out."

Rebecca pushed her eggs around on her plate. Tony barely made a dent in his omelet. With the coffee growing cold, the ice melting in their water glasses, Tony finally called for the check.

As they descended from the foothills into the Sacramento Valley, Rebecca took in a decade's worth of changes she'd barely noticed when she'd first arrived just over a month ago. Empty hillsides had been filled with houses. Big box stores, strip malls and hotels had sprouted up in what had once been rolling pastureland. Sacramento itself had changed little, only a few new buildings catching her eye. As they drew nearer their old neighborhood, the familiarity flooded her.

"I thought we'd go by Estelle's old place first," Tony said.

She welcomed the delay. As powerful as the urgency was to see again the place they'd laid their son to rest, at the same time she dreaded the first moment she saw that small stone. She knew that grief waited for her there. Maybe this short side trip would give her the time to build up a modicum of defense against it.

But as they pulled onto 15th Street, then into the alley that the old house fronted, her emotions jumbled even further. Her first glimpse of the old Victorian where she'd spent a year of her life brought her close to tears.

Tony took her hand. "They've kept it up well."

The clapboards were a dazzling white, the trim a vibrant blue. The house crowded the narrow lot, shouldered up into the sky with a tall peaked roof centered by a dormer window facing the street. Rebecca had spent many an afternoon staring out that window through the thickly leafed red maple.

She scanned the railed front porch. The porch swing was gone, replaced by two redwood chairs. "When did she sell it?"

"A year ago. She'd seen her last foster daughter off to college and was debating whether to take on any more children. Then I told her what I had in mind for an independent living program and she decided it was time to give up the house."

"It had to be hard living here after Jake died." Estelle's husband had been funny and patient and kind.

Tony started the Suburban again and pulled back onto 15th Street. "Any interest in seeing your old place?"

A few years ago, her parents had sold their three-bedroom ranch in Rancho Cordova and bought a condo in San Diego. "With Mom and Dad gone, it doesn't hold much meaning to me."

As they made their way down J Street, Tony glanced over at her. "I would have thought you would have come for Jake's funeral."

"I wanted to." Desperately. She'd cried when her mother had finally reached her two days after the memorial service. "Phillip and I were on a belated honeymoon in Baja."

Tony's jaw worked at the mention of Phillip. "Why belated?"

"We were working hard setting up a new restaurant for an investor. Where I worked before I came here. We just couldn't find the time to get away."

"So you worked with your ex."

As they passed under the Capital City Freeway, her skin prickled. They'd followed this route from Estelle's the morning of Alejandro's funeral. They'd gone to St. Mary's first for the service, then to the cemetery.

"We met at a funky little diner in Beverly Hills. We both wanted to open our own place, but neither one of us had the wherewithal to put a deal together. Phillip met a film producer who'd opened one restaurant and wanted another, more upscale place. He hired Phillip as manager and Phillip hired me."

They turned onto Alhambra, the Sunday traffic minimal on the usually busy thoroughfare. One more turn onto Folsom, then in less than a mile West Hills Cemetery would be on their right. Every muscle in her body seemed to lock down in anticipation.

When Tony reached for her, taking her hand from her lap, she barely registered the contact. Navigating one-handed, he turned the Suburban into the entrance, slowing on the narrow roadway. Verdant green lawns stretched out in all directions, a stark contrast to the yellow, summer-crisped hillsides they'd passed along Highway 50. Towering oaks, redwoods and cedars dotted the landscape, creating an achingly beautiful vista.

Her throat felt so tight, she could barely breathe. The first several months, while her marriage withered and died, she'd come here nearly every day. Learned the shape of every tree, had memorized the names on the markers ringing Alejandro's. In the decade-plus since she'd left, the images should have blurred, become more difficult to recall. But she might as well have had a photo album spread on her lap, so crystal clear was each picture in her mind.

When Tony finally pulled up to the curb, she thought her heart would jolt from her chest. He had to peel her fingers away from his so he could climb from the truck. When he opened her door for her, she groped for him again, fearing her knees would give way without him to anchor her.

"How can he forgive me?" she asked, tears choking her throat. "For being gone so long?" She gasped in a breath. "How can he forgive me for abandoning him?"

Rebecca's words plunged a dagger of pain into Tony's chest, stealing the air from his lungs. For a single, selfish moment, he wanted to shout at her, *It was me you abandoned. Me and our marriage.* Then he felt ashamed. Whatever criticism Rebecca deserved about walking out on him, this wasn't the time or place.

Pushing aside his anger, he drew her into his arms. "You didn't abandon our son, sweetheart. He's been in your heart all along. Right where he should be."

"Why couldn't I come back?" she asked, her mouth moving against the thin fabric of his dress shirt. "I wanted to. So many times, I made plans, booked a flight. But I didn't…I couldn't…" She gasped, then squeezed out in a whisper, "What's wrong with me?"

"Nothing, sweetheart, nothing." He set her back from him so he could meet her gaze. "He isn't here, Becca. His spirit is in heaven. He knows how much you loved him."

She stared at him for a long moment, then lifted her hand and pressed it against his cheek.

He bent to kiss her forehead, the feel of her sun-warmed skin tugging him back in time. Then he pulled away. He handed her the vase of flowers and the palm-sized teddy bear. She hugged both to her chest.

"Give me just a sec," he told her.

He opened the Suburban's back door and reached across for the bulging plastic bag he'd left there. With the bag hooked across his wrist, he took the vase from her and linked his fingers with hers. They walked across the cool grass, in and out of the dappled shade of oaks, maples and elm, crepe myrtle and sequoias, retracing a path they'd followed together twelve years ago.

"Do you remember where it is?" he asked her, then realized the question was unnecessary. She was headed un- erringly toward Alejandro's headstone, fifth row, third from the right. The memorial park had named this section of the cemetery *Baby Lane,* a heartbreaking identification.

She dropped to her knees just below the flat headstone, unmindful of what the damp grass might do to her delicate skirt. At first her hands hovered in the air, then she folded herself, and, setting aside the bear, she lowered her palms to the carved granite set flush with the earth. Her fingers traced the letters with exquisite care—Alejandro Herrera— then grazed the single date for both birth and death.

Steadying the vase and bag in the grass, he knelt beside her, the moist green lawn soaking into his dark trousers. If he couldn't get his pants clean again, he'd buy a new pair; what mattered was being close to Rebecca.

He laid his hand on her back, drawing soothing circles. Her fingers were spread across the dark stone, covering the heart they'd had engraved below Alejandro's name.

"I thought it would hurt more, being here," she said softly.

"It's peaceful. He feels closer here."

She looked up at him over her shoulder, her eyes filled with tears. "We had so many dreams for him."

Late at night, lying in each other's arms, they'd spin out a marvelous future for their much-loved child. He would play ball with his father, pick wildflowers for his mother. Go to college, do important work, marry and have children of his own.

"It wasn't meant to be." He forced out the platitude.

"If only…" She sighed. "If I hadn't…"

He said more gently, "It wasn't meant to be."

She straightened then, wiping her tears away. She took the vase and set it in one corner of the stone, then propped the bear up against it.

"What's in the bag?" she asked.

He brought it over so she could see. "I like to bring… gifts, I guess you could call them. For all of them." He gestured at the rows of headstones in Baby Lane. "I went down to the dollar store in town yesterday."

He opened the bag, showed her what he'd bought. "Toy cars for the boys, little ponies for the girls."

She gave him a trembling smile. "Can I help you?"

He rolled down the edges of the bag and she took a handful of the ponies. They walked along the rows of headstones, some flat like Alejandro's, some upright. Rebecca set a pony in the grass beside each girl's marker; Tony placed a toy car beside the boys'. The ritual he'd followed during most of his visits here, the giving of gifts, took on greater depth and meaning with Rebecca at his side. He could imagine Alejandro, a sturdy boy of nearly twelve, watching them and approving.

The extras he'd bought—he never wanted to take the

chance of coming up short—he wrapped up in the plastic bag for another trip. Then they stood over Alejandro's grave one last time. Rebecca's whispered "I love you" was so soft, it could have been a breeze sifting through the towering redwood above them.

His arm around her shoulders, hers around his waist, they returned to the Suburban. He opened the door for her, put out a hand to help her step up.

She closed his hand in both of hers. Lifting it to her mouth, she kissed the backs of his fingers. "Thank you. What you've given me today…" She squeezed his hand. "Thank you."

A reverent silence settled around them as they drove home. Deep in Tony's heart, a spark of forgiveness flared.

Chapter Ten

Wednesday afternoon, Rebecca had just stretched out on her bed for a much-needed nap before dinner prep, when a soft knock rattled her door. Squinting against the sunshine spilling through the lightweight curtains, she elbowed herself up off the pillows. "Yes?"

"It's Colleen. Do you have a minute?"

Rebecca flopped back on her bed, sorely tempted to say no. It had been a rough few days since the visit to Alejandro's grave. Between that and the heightened anxiety of the teens as opening weekend approached, Rebecca had felt rubbed raw. The last thing she wanted to deal with was another episode of hormonal drama.

She levered herself upright, pushing aside the light blanket she'd pulled over her. "Come in."

Colleen slipped inside, then shut the door. She dropped

into the armchair up against Rebecca's dresser. Tucking her long brown hair behind her ears, Collen locked slender fingers in her lap.

"I was wondering…" Her gaze fell to her hands, her fingers restless. "You and Tony…" She shrugged. "Do you think it was a mistake? That you shouldn't have gotten together?"

Sunday night's discussion had omitted any mention of Rebecca's pregnancy. She and Tony had wanted to maintain at least that one bit of privacy.

"We thought we were in love," she told Colleen. "I don't know if I'd call that a mistake."

The girl's dark head dipped in a nod. "But you didn't stay married. Do you think…" Hands propped under her chin, she directed her blue eyes at Rebecca. "Was it that you didn't really love him? That you only thought you did? Or did you…stop loving him?"

"That's awfully personal, Colleen."

"I know." She looked down again. "I stick my nose in where I shouldn't. That's what my mom—my real mom— would say. When I was little, she'd be gone all night and I'd ask where she was. She'd hit me."

She recounted her mother's abuse in such an offhand tone of voice. Rebecca's heart ached in sympathy.

What could the truth hurt? "I did love him. I just think I didn't understand everything that marriage entailed. What it took to keep a husband and wife together."

"But if you loved him—"

"Love isn't always enough. It should be, but sometimes…life puts up barriers."

Would those barriers defeat her now? She thought not—she was stronger than that younger woman. She even thought that if the bridges hadn't been so thoroughly burned between her and Tony, they might be able to re-create a life together.

If she still loved him. If he still loved her.

"I've been through a lot," Colleen said, pulling Rebecca out of her reverie. "I think barriers would be no big deal for me."

"You're young, sweetheart. You have plenty time to figure out what's right for you." Rebecca took Colleen's hand and gave it a squeeze. "Don't worry about what happened with me and Tony. You're a different person with a different life."

"We are." With a dazzling smile, Colleen shook her hand. "Thanks, Rebecca." She hurried out the door, her step much lighter than when she'd entered.

Sliding from the bed, Rebecca fumbled for the shoes she'd left on the floor. She'd never sleep now, not with her conversation with Colleen roiling in her mind. She might as well walk over to the bakeshop, get an early start on dinner setup.

Tying the laces on her white, rubber-soled shoes, she tried to shake off what she'd seen in Colleen's young face. She'd seen herself in that hopeful optimism, the indelible belief that love conquers all. She'd been that girl once, had built everything around love's promise. That foundation had fallen away, leaving her life in a shambles.

No one's fault. A genetic defect no one could have predicted, a death that every best effort had proved insufficient against.

Shaking off the past yet again, Rebecca scooped her hair back in a ponytail as she left her room. Down the hall, Jana's door was cracked open a few inches. Her hand up to knock, to let Jana know she was on her way to the kitchen, Rebecca hesitated as Jana's voice rose to a panicked near shout.

"How can you just go?" A few second's pause, then, "Ian, you know I can't."

Unwilling to step into yet another drama, Rebecca withdrew. She could speak with Jana later, see if the girl needed some moral support, but for the moment she had enough of her own heartache to process. She closed the cottage door quietly behind her.

As summer crawled into early September, the days had grown shorter, the merciless heat forced to meet a shorter deadline before it gave up its grip on the daylight hours. At three-thirty, the sun already slanted through the trees, striping the gravel path with nascent autumnal shadows.

Her gaze on the sun-dappled trees, she didn't see Tony until she collided with him on the path. As her hands flew up against his chest, he took hold of her shoulders.

Her fingers curled against his knit shirt. "Sorry."

"You seemed a million miles away."

A million years away. With his steadying hands wrapped around her arms, her reminiscences tangled with the present. The feel of Tony under her palms in the afternoon sunlight overlay memories of stealing midnight kisses at Estelle's. Everything had been so simple then. They loved each other, wanted to spend their lives together. Nothing stood in their way.

His hands drifted down her arms. She wanted to rise up on tiptoe to press her lips against his, to see if she could recapture the long-ago connection between them. But did she truly want to return to the girl she was then? Revisit the boy she knew all those years ago? Neither one of them had been strong enough to face life together.

He let go of her, his fingers lingering at her wrists a moment before he stepped back. "What did Colleen want?"

"How did you know she was at the cottage?"

A faint flush rose in his cheeks. "I saw her through my office window."

She remembered the window that faced the cottage. Filing cabinets to one side, the copier on a bookcase underneath it. An awkward place to stand to look at the view.

"I appreciate you watching out for me." His solicitude since the day in the cemetery had added another layer of turmoil to her emotions. "I'm fine, really."

"I'll walk you to the bakeshop and you can tell me about Colleen."

They moved on down the path. "Nothing to tell. We talked about love."

"She's eighteen. I would think she'd know everything there is to know about love." As they reached the kitchen door, he pulled out his key. "Didn't we?"

"We thought we did."

His key in the lock, he stared at her. "You don't think it was real?"

In that moment, emotion rested so heavily inside her that exhaustion swamped her. "I don't know anymore, Tony."

When she wished he'd open the door then leave, he stepped inside with her and shut the door. "Something I wanted to talk over with you."

"Is Lea still having trouble sleeping?" Too edgy to stand still, she headed toward the dry stores.

He followed her into the small, shelf-lined alcove. "Six days without a nightmare."

"That's good."

The sunshine spilling through the kitchen windows cast a dim light in the dry stores, just bright enough to see the stacks of paper goods, dry pasta and canned tomatoes lining the shelves. It also gave the cramped space an intimate feel with Tony standing so close. She wanted to turn on the fluorescents, but she would have to reach past him to flip the switch and risk touching him.

She stared blindly at a row of canned beans, trying to recall why she came in here. "If the problem's not Lea, then what?"

He leaned against a shelf, his broad shoulders filling her field of view. "I've received applications from two girls who are about to be aged out of the foster system."

"I could fit them into the cooking program." She put her hands on the boxes of pasta to avoid putting them on him. "It would give our current group a chance to do some training themselves. But where would you house them?"

"That's the problem. The only space is the downstairs bedroom in the main house. It's small, but I could squeeze two in there."

"Except—"

"I can't share the house with students," Tony said. "Certainly not the girls. And with Lea, I wouldn't feel comfortable housing the boys there, either."

"Jana and I could double up in the cottage. Put two of the girls in the other room."

"Not enough space. It was a small bedroom to start with before I divided it for you and Jana."

"What about Estelle's room?" It had been the foreman's

back in the days when Estelle's House was a working ranch and was larger than the others.

He shook his head. "I'm not asking Estelle to give up her space. It's enough that she sold her house to move here. The other rooms are barely big enough for two."

A perfect solution drifted into her mind. When her gaze met Tony's she realized he'd come to the same conclusion. A trembling trailed lazily up her spine. "You want me and Jana to move into the house."

"If you wouldn't mind. You'd have to share the room with Jana, which would mean less privacy for both of you."

But it also meant a built-in buffer between her and Tony. With Jana in the house, they didn't dare risk any misstep that would set the gossip mill into action.

"Jana's in her room now if you want to ask her. I'm sure she won't mind the change in living quarters."

He straightened. "I'd like to get back to these applicants ASAP. They both have to be out by the day after Labor Day. They have nowhere else to go."

She expected him to leave, to finally give her a chance to breathe again. But instead he came nearer, laid his hand against her cheek. "Thank you."

His smile sent her heart rocketing in her chest. His dark gaze scanned her face, dropped to her mouth. Without a single thought as to the consequences, she reached for him. Her eyes fluttered closed as he lowered his head, his lips scudding across hers.

His hand against her back, he pulled her closer, urging her against him. She wrapped her arms around him, wanting to feel every inch of his body against hers. In the last few days, everything had seemed a jumble, so little made sense. But Tony in her arms, kissing her, holding her, was like a brilliant illumination in the blackest of rooms.

He walked her backward, deeper inside the dry stores. If anyone happened into the kitchen, they wouldn't see her and Tony in the alcove. With the light off, no one would think to look inside.

"I've tried so damn hard not to touch you." His words caressed her ear even as his mouth pressed kisses along the sensitive whorls. "You've been so fragile since Sunday."

"This makes me feel stronger." Her breath caught as his tongue trailed a moist path down her throat. "I never thought I could forget the grief, but you—" His palm centered on her breast, teased her nipple through her shirt. "You give me something new."

He cradled her face with both hands. "We're not going anywhere, Becca. You and me—our time is past."

"I know." She turned her head to kiss the rampant pulse in his wrist. "I don't want to go back. And there's no going forward, either." Regret weighted her heart.

"As long as we both know." One hand drifting down her body again, he kissed her. "When do the kids show up?"

"Another twenty minutes."

"Enough time, then."

"It'll have to do."

He tugged her shirt up, freeing it inch by inch. Once he had it loosened, his hand moved lazily under and splayed across her rib cage. His thumb rested just below the curve of her breast, stroking in arcs closer, then away, teasing her.

As his hand warmed her, his mouth explored her face, brushing kisses across her cheeks, along her jaw. His teeth closed gently around the lobe of her ear, scraping. His tongue traced the shell of her ear, sending shivers down her spine.

"Not enough time to do everything I want," he whispered.

Then as she wondered what he intended, his hand shifted back down to the waistband of her slacks. His fingertips dipped inside, releasing the button with one clever motion. As he lowered the zipper, she grabbed his wrist, tried to stop him. He twisted free, blocking her with his other hand as his fingers dove past the elastic of her panties.

"We did more than this on Estelle's back porch," he murmured. "I watched you fall apart long before you could ever return the favor." He drew circles on the tender skin of her belly, moving lower with each circuit.

Her heart pounded in her ear. "What if someone arrives early?"

"Have they ever?"

She shook her head, feeling her knees weaken.

"Then let me do this, Becca. I've been wanting to for so damn long."

She felt the first gentle intrusion into the thick dark curls at the apex of her thighs. Then his fingers brushed lightly against her cleft. She relaxed her legs with little urging, allowing his knee between them. All the while, he kissed her, his tongue tasting the line of her jaw, the corner of her mouth.

His finger prodded between her folds, found the aching tenderness between them. She'd forgotten how to feel this way with Tony. No one had ever reached her the way he had. The way he did now. He explored deeper between her legs, then as his tongue thrust inside her mouth, his finger matched the movement deep inside her. Her moan of pleasure spilled into his mouth as his palm pressed hard against her. The circles he'd drawn before collapsed into a smaller motion that centered on her exquisitely sensitive nub. Her hands fell to her sides, gripping the edge of the shelf behind her as she struggled to keep herself upright.

He slipped a second finger inside, thrusting in and out as he rubbed his palm against her. She was eighteen again, an innocent young girl ready to give herself to the boy she loved under a night sky glittering with stars.

The pressure of his hand, his clever fingers, sent her over the edge in a waterfall of exultation she had no defense against. Her body throbbed around his fingers, tightening, holding him in place. Wetness like warm honey soaked his hand, and she wanted desperately to feel his erection inside her. But he pulled away, one arm still around her waist to support her.

"No time," he whispered. "Damn it."

One last kiss, then he stroked a lock of her hair behind her ear. She tucked in her shirt, zipped her slacks, her cheeks hot as she looked up at him. "We shouldn't have done that," she said softly.

She didn't miss his smugness, his unrepentant expression. "There were a lot of things we shouldn't have done on Estelle's porch."

She couldn't help but smile. She reached up to cup her hand against his face. "I would have thought we were old enough to know better."

He laughed. "We are."

He bent to kiss her again, but the rattle of the kitchen door interrupted. By the time Serena, Ruby and Ari entered, Tony had moved to the sink to wash his hands. Rebecca had her clothes tidied and her hair pulled back into its ponytail. She filled her hands with boxes of linguini before she stepped into view of the teens.

From the door he called out, "I'll go talk to Jana," then left her to face the avid gazes of the three girls.

She ignored the questions in their eyes. "Linguini with white clam sauce. Very easy pantry meal. Serena, get a pot of water going. Ruby, grab two lemons from the walk-in. Ari, I'll need you to make a salad...."

Tony went to the house first, heading straight for the downstairs bathroom. His body was on fire, filled with one driving need—Rebecca, touching her, kissing her, holding her. A cold shower might be sufficient to soothe him long enough to make it through the afternoon and evening—if the water was arctic and the dousing hours long.

Instead, he soaked his head in the sink, running handfuls of water over his face and hair. Then he straightened and saw himself in the mirror, took in the crazed look of his reflection. He'd damn well better find a way to get through his conversation with Jana without scaring the poor girl to death.

Scrubbing himself dry, he boxed up the heated memories that raced through his mind. He refused to let himself think about Rebecca's scent, the feel of her, the sounds she'd made as she came. He had a discussion to get through with Jana and work to finish before dinner.

He headed out the door, his body still wound tight as a drum, wondering how the hell he'd get through dinner tonight. How he'd be able to think about anything but what had happened in the dry stores. How to keep from calculating ways to get Rebecca alone so they could finish what they'd started.

To give himself a little more cooldown time before facing Jana, he stopped at his office. There'd been some data missing from one of the applicants' intake forms. She'd promised to e-mail the requested information.

As he scanned his e-mail inbox, he spotted a message with the subject line, *Cooking Instruction Position*. He'd completely forgotten he'd posted notices for a replacement for Rebecca on a few online job sites. It had taken so long to find someone suitable the first time, he'd wanted to give himself a good head start.

Clicking the e-mail open, he read enough of the woman's message to realize she all but matched Rebecca's professional experience, including years spent mentoring foster children. A resident of Boise, Idaho, she was willing to relocate to be closer to family. She could start as early as December, when her current contract ended.

He'd told Rebecca at the outset her tenure would only be five months. Since then, he'd done nothing to find someone to take her place except the ads on the Web. In the month since he'd posted them, this was the first viable response.

Typing a response asking the woman to call him for a phone interview, he left the office and continued on toward the cottage. It took Jana a long time to open the door.

"Did I wake you from a nap?" he asked her.

"No. Yes. Not really." She ran her fingers through her short, spiky hair. "Did you want to come in?"

When he stepped past her, he was surprised to see her eyes were red-rimmed, as if she'd been crying. He made a mental note to ask Rebecca to speak to her. "I'd like to bring two new girls into the program." He explained to her about the possible change in living arrangements.

"Sure." She shrugged. "Whatever. I don't mind sharing with Rebecca."

What was up with Jana? Sometimes brash, sometimes irreverent, she was always upbeat. Maybe he ought to ask her himself what was going on.

He would have, if Estelle and Lea hadn't turned up just then. "Changing of the guard," Estelle said as Lea ran over to Jana.

Jana bent to pick up Lea, hugging her tightly. "I sure love you, sweetpea." She closed her eyes a moment, then looked over at Tony. "Would it be okay if I took off early Friday?"

"That's the day before opening. I might need you to watch Lea."

Guilt flickered in her face.

"Ian and I...have something to do."

"Would you be coming back Friday night?"

She kept her gaze on Lea. "No."

"I can keep an eye on Lea on Friday." Estelle leaned against the doorjamb, releasing a tired sigh. "But you don't want to miss opening day on Saturday."

"I won't." Jana gave Lea a kiss, then carried the little girl out the door. "Let's take a walk, sweetpea."

Tony exchanged a look with Estelle. "What was that all about?"

Estelle narrowed her gaze on Jana's retreating back. "A fight with Ian?"

Maybe that's what the early departure on Friday was all about—she wanted a chance to work things out with her boyfriend. Not the best excuse for a day off, but at least she'd asked rather than just not show up.

KAREN SANDLER   137

They locked up and left the cottage. As he walked her to the bunkhouse, Tony threw an arm around Estelle's shoulders. Damn, she was thin. Her proportions had always been generous—she was built for comfort, not speed, she liked to say. As a boy, he'd loved her pillowy hugs.

Now he felt the boniness of her shoulders, the frailty of her. Thank God she'd be seeing her doctor in a few days.

Her canny gaze fixed on him. "How are things going with you and Rebecca?"

With the mere mention of her name, the images came crowding back, apparently marching right across his face. Estelle laughed. "Like that, is it?"

He could feel himself blush like a schoolboy. "We're not…"

"Never mind." Estelle flapped a hand at him, a broad smile on her face.

He had to sink Estelle's notion that there was some chance of a reunion between him and Rebecca. The e-mail he'd received provided the perfect ammunition. "I may have found a replacement."

"For who?"

"Rebecca. I got a résumé from a woman who'd be perfect for the job."

"Rebecca is already perfect." At the bunkhouse door, Estelle seemed to grow a couple inches with indignation.

He was a grown man, yet he still feared Estelle's disapproval. Not to mention her wrath when she was riled.

But they'd agreed personnel issues would be his decision. "Rebecca's a short-timer. That's been the understanding from the start."

Estelle's gaze narrowed. "Whose understanding?"

"Mine. And Rebecca's." Except the short term to her employment had been his idea.

Estelle went from indignant to fierce. "You can't just pull the rug out from under these kids by sending Rebecca away."

"I won't." He patted her shoulder awkwardly. "The replacement wouldn't start until the next session. This group of kids will have moved on."

"And Rebecca's on board with this?" Estelle asked, suspicion clear in her tone.

He felt as he had as a boy when Estelle had caught him in a lie. Even though leaving at the end of this session was exactly what Rebecca had agreed to, he couldn't quite bring himself to say yes.

"I haven't even talked to the woman yet. The interview might not pan out. No point in getting ahead of ourselves."

He hugged her goodbye, then walked away, feeling her watching him until the turn in the path. He might as well have been a kid again, the candy bar he'd lifted from the corner market melting in his pocket, Estelle waiting on the porch for him.

He'd all but thrown himself at her feet that day. When she'd passed her sentence—sweeping the floors of that store for a month, both after school and on the weekends. He'd almost wept with gratitude. Because it could have been worse. She could have sent him away.

As he intended to do with Rebecca. It wasn't the same. She was an adult, he'd been a kid. It wasn't as if she wouldn't have a dozen places she could land after leaving here.

But he knew that in Estelle's eyes, it still wasn't right.

Chapter Eleven

"Katy, there should be nine coffee cakes, not eight!" Rebecca shouted as she hurried through the kitchen, her arms loaded with packages of napkins. She tossed the packages one at a time to James in the dining room, who passed them, relay-style, to Kevin.

"Those were the only ones marked *Saturday* I could find," Katy said. "I dug clear to the back of the freezer."

Rebecca checked the kitchen clock. A quarter after nine, only forty-five minutes until opening. "Look again. Those cakes will sell fast."

Katy flounced off to the chest freezer in the back, her usual smile missing. Rebecca strafed the dining room with her gaze, assessing the setup.

"James, Kevin, did you wipe down all the tables?"

"Just the ones we've been using," Kevin told her.

"I want them all wiped. The stored tables have been gathering dust. James, you clean the chairs."

"All of them?" He stared at her in shock.

"Every one."

James zoomed into the kitchen, no doubt in search of a bucket and clean rag, just as Tony was heading for the door with a tray full of plastic tumblers. Rebecca saw the impending collision an instant before it happened, covering her face in reaction as the tumblers scattered across the floor. Tony barked out a four-letter word she'd only heard him use when they were making love, then stepped back, lips moving as he silently counted to ten.

James, crouching to pick up the fallen water cups, grinned up at Tony. "Good thing you sent Lea over to stay with Grams."

Ruby, busy slicing the coffee cakes into portions with Serena, called out, "We're gonna have to wash your mouth out with soap, Tony."

"Do we need to put you in the time-out chair?" Ari yelled. She gestured with a pair of apple turnovers she'd pulled from a foil-wrapped pan.

Colleen took the pastries from Ari and stacked them on a cake plate. "I think he oughta put a dollar in the cuss jar for that one."

Tony laughed, grabbing the tumblers from James as the boy passed them up to him. They worked together to get the plasticware in the dishwasher for a rewashing as the banter continued around them, the girls scolding Tony, adding on ever-more preposterous punishments for his transgression.

Grinning, he looked back over his shoulder at Rebecca and she thought her heart would stop. Their encounter in the dry stores room replayed with Technicolor clarity in her mind. They hadn't exchanged a word about what had happened—after moving into the main house a couple of days ago, living under Jana and Lea's noses, they hadn't had so much as a moment alone together. Not to mention Tony being so busy getting everything set up for the arrival of the two new students after Labor Day. But every touch had burned deep into Rebecca's body, leaving her sleepless and restless late into the night.

The message he broadcast to her now turned her knees to water. She all but felt his fingers moving along her skin, his breath hot on her cheek. She forced herself to turn away, then spent several seconds trying to remember what she'd planned to do next.

She hollered toward the back of the kitchen, where Katy was still buried in the chest freezer. "Did you fall in, Katy? Let's go!"

Katy finally emerged with the last coffee cake clutched to her chest. She glanced out the small window beside the freezer, then turned toward Rebecca with a look of total panic on her face. "Someone's pulled into the parking lot. We don't even open for another half hour."

The other girls raced toward the window, Brittany leading the pack. "Ohmigod, he's got a DeLorean," she squealed. "I've never seen one except in movies."

"That'll be Sam Harrison." Tony pulled the last tray of steaming tumblers from their sterilizing bath in the dishwasher. If he'd been affected by the look that had passed between them, you couldn't hear it in his voice. "I asked him to come early."

Now the herd of girls thundered back to the front of the kitchen and into the dining room, Ruby more excited than

Rebecca had ever seen her. "Sam Harrison, the writer? I've got all his books."

While the girls clustered around the dining-room door, the boys jockeying for position behind them, Tony beckoned to Rebecca. "He's been looking forward to seeing you."

"He was always a good friend."

She could still remember his grave expression the night he'd picked her up for the drive to the airport. *Are you sure, Becca?* he'd asked. She'd told him yes, although she hadn't been certain of anything.

They squeezed through the mass of teens out the door. The Saturday of Labor Day weekend had dawned with the first crisp coolness of fall, a perfect clear blue sky arching overhead. The leaves still clinging to the oaks had dulled, but it was still too early for them to fall.

Sam leaned against the silver gull-wing door of his car, looking around him at the ranch. He smiled as they drew nearer, pushing off from the sleek sports car and spreading out his arms to take Rebecca in a hug.

"Damn, it's good to see you. You look great."

He let her go, then shook Tony's hand. His height topped Tony's by a good six inches. Although he'd never been anything but a friend to Rebecca, she had to admit he was drop-dead gorgeous with his black Irish looks. At thirty-four, he was four years older than her, but in the eleven years since she'd seen him last, time had only improved his face.

When she looked back at Tony, she saw the speculation in his face and a glimmer of something that astounded her—possessiveness. He angled closer to her, putting himself between her and Sam.

Sam laughed, throwing up his hands. "Hey, no worries. I wouldn't dream of intruding on your territory."

She waited for Tony to correct Sam, to let him know there was nothing between him and her. Then she remembered what had happened in the dry stores, and she wasn't sure what was right anymore.

Tony clapped a hand on Sam's shoulder. "Come see what your money built."

"Is Jana around?" Sam asked as they started toward the entrance to the bakeshop. "She was begging me for a copy of my new book. I have it in the car."

"She's off with her boyfriend today," Tony told him. "Should be back before you leave, though."

The teens spilled from the dining room as Sam approached. Ruby gazed up at him in adoration, Kevin and James peppered him with questions about the DeLorean and the rest of his collection of rare cars. Brittany, Serena and Ari buzzed around him, openly flirting.

Sam took it all in stride. "You all can check out the car later, if there's time."

"Thanks for the offer, Sam," Rebecca said, "but these kids will be lucky to take a breath today, let alone go joyriding."

James deflated with disappointment. Sam patted him on the back. "Another time." He turned to Tony. "I was able to touch base with my publicist. She arranged for some press coverage today."

Katy, lagging behind, took another look out the door. "A TV news van just pulled in." Her mouth dropped open. "Ohmigod, we're gonna be on television."

By the bakeshop's six o'clock closing time, the teens were running on fumes, Lea was all but bouncing off the walls and Tony had spent far too many hours contemplating the use of caramel sauce on Rebecca's naked body. He'd made more than one trip into the walk-in for no other reason than to cool his jets, to remind himself that not every word out of Rebecca's mouth was the invitation to sex his libido seemed to think it was.

She just plain overwhelmed him. She seemed to possess an endless well of energy, keeping her head with each meltdown, juggling a hundred balls at once without losing track of one. She'd impressed the hell out of the reporter, and the cameraman kept ogling her, despite her modest white blouse and apron.

He wondered if Helen Franks, the potential replacement he'd interviewed by phone yesterday morning, could have put in as stellar a performance. Helen had sounded perfect for the job, but Rebecca would leave some enormous shoes to fill.

If he could let her leave at all.

Estelle had brought Lea over at four o'clock, telling him his daughter couldn't stand to be the only one left out of the fun. He took one look at Estelle, the circles under her eyes, the sallowness of her skin, and told her to go lie down. Her Tuesday doctor appointment couldn't come too soon.

He'd tried to reach Jana on her cell, to see if she could return and keep an eye on Lea, but had to leave a voice mail when Jana didn't answer. He hadn't heard a peep from her since she'd left yesterday at noon. When he asked, none of the girls had heard from her either, not even Katy, who'd made a particular connection with his assistant. Even though Saturday was Jana's day off, he could usually reach her if he needed her.

Rebecca took Lea's addition to the mix in stride, giving

her small tasks to do to keep her out of the way—reloading sugar and sweetener packets in their plastic holders and coffee creamers in small serving bowls. Sam pitched in as well, keeping one eye on Lea while he kept up with the steady flow of dirty dishes. Scullery wasn't the job Tony would have chosen for Estelle's House's main benefactor, but Sam had insisted—might as well make use of all those years working through high school as a busboy.

At six o'clock, there was nothing left on the counters but two apple turnovers, one squished poached pear and pans full of coffee cake crumbs. Other than the pear, nothing had gone to waste; in fact, they'd had to dip into some of Sunday's stock when the peach cobbler ran out.

Kevin and Colleen saw the last customers out and locked the front door. As they all gathered in the kitchen, Tony looked out over the ragtag group he'd assembled just over a month ago.

"Damn, I'm proud of you."

Ruby laughed and grabbed for the cuss jar. She shook it. "Cough up, Tony."

Grinning, he dug a quarter from his pocket and tossed it in the jar. "You know who you have to thank for this."

They all turned to Rebecca, standing near the dishwasher with Ari and Serena on either side of her, an arm around each of them. In the next moment, she vanished as all eight of them enfolded her in a group hug. When they released her and she came up for air, she swiped tears from her eyes.

"It was your own hard work," she said, her gaze falling on each of the teens in turn. "You all made this a success." She stepped around Ari to link an arm with Sam. "Don't forget this guy's contribution."

The girls came over to give Sam a hug and the boys to

shake his hand. As Rebecca smiled up at him, a spurt of jealousy burned inside Tony, as crazy now as it had been earlier today when he'd caught her admiring Sam's damned good looks. He wanted to take her hand and pull her away from Sam, to hold her against his own side. When Sam leaned down to whisper something to her, Tony had to tamp down the impulse to say something.

Then she looked over at him, her eyes still damp. Her tender expression curled around his heart and gave it a tug. She could have been nineteen again, both of them with their whole lives ahead of them.

Rebecca smiled at her crew. "There's still some clean-up to do, some prep for tomorrow. But I think you've all earned a little recess—if you're still interested in taking a look at Sam's DeLorean?"

James and Kevin all but mowed each other down racing for the door. The girls gathered around Sam as he followed, Ruby beside him asking earnest questions about his writing process. Lea hung back, hovering beside Rebecca.

"Colleen will keep an eye on you, honey, if you want to go," Rebecca told his daughter.

Lea fidgeted with Rebecca's pinky finger. "I want to see the car. Sam says it has wings."

"Then I think you should see it." Rebecca took Lea's hand. "I'll take you out to Colleen."

There was no missing the adoration in Lea's face as she walked alongside Rebecca. He'd known they'd risk Lea becoming attached to Rebecca if she stayed, but he'd thought that as Lea grew more confident, she'd be able to become more independent of her. But if anything, the connection between his daughter and Rebecca became more tightly woven every day. He also suspected she was no longer a substitute for Elena in Lea's heart, but a loved one in her own right.

And what did he feel for her? Physically, the answer was a no-brainer. He wanted Rebecca in his bed. He wanted to make love to her for hours, revisit all the ways he once took her to heaven, discover new routes to ecstasy. If not for Jana sharing Rebecca's room, he'd be down there with her every night, taking her body naked under his, reveling in the feel of himself inside her.

She returned to the kitchen, pulling off her apron and tossing it into the laundry bag. "I've been ordered out of my own kitchen. The kids told me they can finish cleanup and setup."

"What about Lea?" he asked as he followed her out the door.

She smiled up at him. "Believe it or not, Colleen persuaded her to spend the night in the bunkhouse. They'll use the boys' old room since they've moved into the cottage already and the new girls haven't arrived yet."

Tension prickled along his spine. "But Jana will be around."

"She should be." She glanced over at the parking lot, no doubt looking for Jana's car. "I would have thought she'd be here before now. She'd wanted to be here for the opening."

As he unlocked the front door and stepped aside to let her in, his chest felt tight. Electricity crackled between them, as if a summer lightning storm had struck in his living room. She wouldn't look at him; he knew if she did, he'd have her in his arms in a heartbeat.

Despite her tiredness, she made it to her bedroom at a

near sprint. He didn't take a breath until she slipped inside and shut the door.

He headed for the stairs, taking them two at a time. Where was Jana? For all her youth, she was usually reliable. He'd wanted her to meet with Sam, discuss some of the additional fund-raising she had planned. Over the last several weeks, she'd built relationships with community liaisons at four or five local corporations. Much as he appreciated Sam's donations, he wanted to let his friend know the burden of financing Estelle's House wasn't entirely on his shoulders.

As he stepped under the shower, the spray spurted and gushed intermittently, a consequence of the elderly water heater and two showers running at once. Which meant Rebecca was in the shower as well, water streaming over her naked body. He remembered all too clearly the silky feel of her wet skin, the way the soap slicked her body. The first time they made love in the shower, Rebecca had been shy and embarrassed. But she'd climaxed in his arms, too weak from exultation to stand on her own.

He twisted the shower control to the left, sucking in a breath as icy water poured over him. It was a temporary fix at best.

He was shivering by the time he finished, trying to keep his mind blank as he dressed in a Hawaiian shirt and jeans. He thought he had himself under control as he descended the stairs—until he spotted Rebecca seated on the living-room sofa, head bent to something in her lap. Just the sight of her, that dark hair with those caramel streaks, her shoulders draped in a raspberry-colored blouse, and all his best intentions flew to the four winds.

He was actually reaching for her as he rounded the

sofa. The troubled expression on her face pulled him up short. "What's wrong?"

She rose, her full floral skirt falling around her hips, all at once shaping and concealing her body. His distracted gaze drifted up to the top button of her blouse, the faint shadow at the vee where the collar fell open.

Then he noticed the piece of printer paper she held out, creased where it had been folded. "It was on my pillow. I didn't see it until I came out of my shower."

He took the paper, recognizing Jana's neat cursive in the few lines written. *I'm sorry, Rebecca, but I have to leave. Ian and I are moving to Oregon.*

Before he could stop himself, he let loose a string of expletives worth at least twenty bucks in the tip jar.

Chapter Twelve

"There's an envelope addressed to me in here," Tony called from the kitchen as Rebecca returned from the bedroom.

"Her dresser's empty. Her closet's cleaned out." She felt heartsick seeing those empty drawers and hangers. She'd grown to like Jana in the time they shared the cottage. "No way of knowing when she packed up, though."

"I can't believe she just up and left."

Worry knotted Rebecca's stomach. "Do you think she was in trouble?"

"She never said a word to me."

"We'll have to ask the kids. Or Sam might know."

Tony bent his head over the paper in his hand, a longer note than the one Jana had left for Rebecca. He turned the sheet toward Rebecca. "A list of names and phone numbers for the folks she's been talking to about donations. At least she didn't leave us completely high and dry."

"She had to have been here today to leave the notes. Likely when the bakeshop was slammed with customers."

With a sigh, Tony leaned against the breakfast bar. "There were a hundred little tasks Jana did during the course of the day, not to mention her watching Lea for me." She could see when the realization struck him. "Damn. What are we going to tell Lea?"

"We'll figure something out."

When he reached for her, she didn't resist, stepping into his embrace. The sensual tension that had simmered between them for days now smoldered like a banked fire tamped for the moment by the crisis of Jana's departure. It would take so little for it to flare up—the slightest pressure of his hand against her back, the faintest kiss brushed against her mouth.

It hit her then—no more Jana, no more built-in chaperone. And with Lea sleeping in the bunkhouse tonight, there was no one to know if Tony spent the night in Rebecca's bed.

She pulled back with a gasp, and she could see from Tony's expression that he'd realized the same thing. His hands wrapped around her arms, flexing as if he struggled against the need to pull her closer again.

She willed herself to step back, and he dropped his hands. "We ought to tell her now. Before she starts asking where Jana is."

They left the house, retracing their path back to the bakeshop. The others were all crowded around one table in the dining room, Katy braiding Serena's hair, Ruby and Ari playing a card game. Lea leaned contentedly against Sam, Estelle on her other side.

But it was the boys' alliances that caused Rebecca to do a double take. James had Brittany snuggled up beside him, not Colleen. And Kevin cradled Colleen in his lap, his cocky grin echoed by her blissful smile.

Rebecca glanced over at Tony, his shrug telling her he didn't know what to make of the change of allegiances, either. "An end to hostilities?" he murmured in her ear.

"I hope so." Her conversation earlier in the week with Colleen now made more sense. But Rebecca had thought the girl was asking about James, not Kevin.

Lea turned and smiled up at her father. "Sam made me a bird out of paper. Look, it flaps its wings, just like his car."

While Tony admired the origami bird, Rebecca took an automatic look around the dining room. Tables were all wiped, napkins and flatware all restocked, tumblers stacked next to the water dispenser ready for tomorrow.

Tony whispered in Estelle's ear, then helped her to her feet. As the two of them walked toward the kitchen, Rebecca saw the worry on several of the teens' faces. Just before she joined Tony and Estelle in the kitchen, she smiled at the students, giving them an okay sign with her fingers.

When Tony gave Estelle the news about Jana, she looked grim, but not surprised.

"It explains her visit earlier today," Estelle said. "She told me she'd decided to stay another night at Ian's and she needed a change of clothes. That he was waiting for her. But she sat with Lea on her lap for a good half hour, reading her a couple of her favorite books. Kept telling her she'd see her soon."

Tony looked through the pass-through at his daughter sitting with Sam. "I guess we should call her in here and tell her. Break it to her before we inform the others."

Estelle put a hand on his arm. "It can wait a day. She's excited about spending the night at the bunkhouse. We don't have to rock her world yet."

Tony glanced over at Rebecca. She answered his silent query. "I agree with Estelle. Tomorrow's soon enough."

When they returned to the dining room, Ruby, Serena, Ari and Katy had lined their chairs up along one side of the table, one behind the other. Serena massaged Ruby's shoulders, Ari worked on Serena and Katy on Ari.

"Sit down, Becca," Ruby called out, hooking a chair with her feet and scooting it in front of her. "I'll do your shoulders."

As Rebecca dropped into the chair, Ari called out, "You should rub her feet, Tony. She's been on 'em all day."

Rebecca would have objected, but Tony pulled over a chair in front of her, seating himself and settling her feet into his lap. With so many eyes on them, there should have been nothing intimate about Tony slipping off her shoes and digging his thumbs into her soles. But while Ruby's brisk massage was friendly, Tony's touch was something else.

She shut her eyes, determined to focus on Ruby's kindness and not the sensual rampage Tony had set off. She sighed as Ruby's fingers dug into a knot in her neck. "I suppose we have to start thinking about dinner."

"Taken care of," Kevin said. "Sam sent out for pizza."

"Except it's not for you and Tony," Ruby said.

"We've all gotta stay here so we can see ourselves on the news. But we decided you two are going out to dinner."

At James's declaration, Rebecca's eyes snapped open. Her gaze locked with Tony's. "We'd be glad to share pizza with all of you."

"Nope," Serena said from behind her. "You two deserve to go out."

"My treat," Sam announced. When Tony opened his mouth to protest, Sam added, "No arguments. And Lea's on board, too."

Lea flapped the wings of her origami bird. "Colleen's gonna read me my bedtime story."

What was the big deal? They'd shared dozens of meals here at the ranch. They'd be in a public restaurant. What could happen?

Nothing in the restaurant, maybe, but afterward, with the two of them alone in the house... She was already breathless with his fingers stroking the arch of her foot, his thigh warm and firm against her skin.

His gaze locked on hers, and she wondered if she'd ever breathe again. She wanted to pull away from Ruby, to curl up in Tony's lap the way Colleen was in Kevin's and wrap her arms around him.

Sam's voice intruded on her fantasy. "I made the reservation for seven-thirty. You two had better get a move on."

Since they'd already showered and changed, Rebecca only had to retrieve her purse from the house. Tony helped her into his truck just as the pizza arrived, the teens spilling from the dining room to help bring it in. As Sam tugged out his wallet to pay, Lea wriggling with excitement beside him, he saluted Tony. Rebecca didn't miss the self-satisfied grin on Sam's face.

Tony didn't know how Sam had arranged it, but the maître d' sat him and Rebecca at the most secluded table in the small, intimate restaurant. Situated in the corner with a strategically placed potted plant shielding them from view—and he wouldn't put it past Sam to have purchased the plant for that express purpose—they might as well have been alone.

Rebecca's soft gaze turned dark and exotic in the dim lighting. "Have you been here before?"

"A bit out of my price range." He looked around at the rustic interior. "It always seemed like the sort a place for special occasions, not a casual meal."

"Is that what we're doing?" she asked, her voice so soft he had to lean closer to hear. Not that he didn't want to lean closer. "Celebrating?"

"I don't think I've wanted to let myself. Not while Lea was still missing. And since Darius returned her to me, with everything so difficult…"

"She's been getting better, though, bit by bit."

"She has." Although there was no telling how she'd react when she learned of Jana's departure.

Rebecca laid her hand over his. "Sometimes you just have to let yourself believe things are okay."

He turned his hand and linked his fingers in hers. "It never seems safe to believe that."

They sat quietly for a long time, waving off the waiter twice. Then Rebecca asked, "How did it happen?"

As often as the ugly story replayed itself in his mind, he was reluctant to relate it out loud. But Elena was gone now, out of reach of Lea.

"I had custody, but she had visitation rights. She was supposed to arrange with me to see Lea, not show up during the day while I was at work."

The au pair he'd hired had been a loving and attentive caregiver. But she didn't see anything wrong with letting Lea see her mother.

"Elena was holding Lea, standing near the door. The au pair literally only turned her back for a moment."

He remembered the terrified call from the young woman, her sobs as she begged Tony's forgiveness. Tony had shouted at her to call the police. When she only cried louder, he'd slammed down the phone and called them himself.

"Going home, seeing her empty room…" It had cut like a knife when he'd stood by her crib. She'd just turned two, and he'd been about to buy her a bed. "I thought when Alejandro died, that was the worst. Then when you left…"

Her gaze dropped, then lifted again to his. "I should have said this to you a long time ago. I never should have left the way I did. To have just walked out—"

"You were young. You were hurting."

"Still, I should have…" She released a long sigh.

"In some ways…" He considered what he wanted to say, to explain the revelation he'd had that day at the cemetery. "In some ways it was for the best. The grief should have brought us closer together, but it didn't. If we'd stayed together, I think we would have just torn each other apart."

Tears gathered in her eyes. "Do you think we didn't love each other enough?"

At the time, he'd thought he'd loved her. That he would have walked through fire for her. But when life slammed him down hard, brought him to his knees, he didn't seem to have enough room in his heart for her. At least not enough to keep her with him.

He pulled free from her and took a sip of water. The ice in the glass rattled as his hand shook. "I look at the kids— Colleen, Kevin, James. At their age, do you think they know what the hell love is? Do you think we did? From one day to the next, Colleen goes from James's arms to Kevin's. If you hadn't gotten pregnant, if we hadn't had to get married, maybe we would have split up just as easily."

Except even as he said the words, they felt like a lie on his tongue. He remembered Kevin that day in his office, the day he and James had nearly torn one another's heads off. The boy had been hurting, desperate for a way to get Colleen back.

"Maybe so." Her movements awkward and jerky, Rebecca unfolded her cloth napkin and spread it on her lap. "But at the time…it felt like love."

She fell silent, and he couldn't think of another thing to say. The waiter came and reeled off a list of specials. They ordered a starter to share and an entrée for each of them. His throat felt so constricted, he wasn't sure how he'd manage to swallow.

He buttered a slice of sourdough just to give himself something to do while they waited for their Thai egg roll to arrive. Rebecca tore the crust off her own bread, but he didn't see her eat any.

Despite their quiet corner, he barely heard her question. "Did you love Elena?"

When he should have had a ready answer, he countered with a query of his own. "Did you love your ex-husband?"

"Phillip?" A faint smile curved her mouth. "We had a lot in common. We respected one another. But he'd told me from the outset he didn't want children. I thought I could live with that, but it ended up being a deal-breaker for me."

"How long were you married?"

"Almost four years. We divorced two years ago."

"There hasn't been anyone else?" He didn't know why he pursued that line of interrogation. He didn't like thinking about her with another man. "Someone more amenable to children?"

"No one. I was fostering a five-year-old girl. The adoption was in progress when Vanessa went back to her mother." She skimmed a finger through the condensation on her water glass. "A couple weeks before I moved up here."

"Then you lost a second child."

She shrugged. "I knew the risk when I took Vanessa in."

"When I first interviewed you, you just about begged me for the job. Was it because of her?"

"Partly. Mostly." She dropped her hands into her lap. "I'd been contemplating a job change for a while, something that would allow me to spend more time with Vanessa. When the adoption fell through, creating high-priced desserts for customers with more money than sense seemed like such a wasted effort."

The waiter brought their egg roll, the scent of curry spicing the air. Rebecca took her half, drawing a circle in the sweet chili sauce with it. "What about Elena?"

He'd sidestepped her question, even now wasn't sure how to answer it. "She was...fragile. The moment I first saw her, I wanted to take care of her."

His heart had all but leapt from his chest when he spotted Elena at Sacramento State the second year of his masters program. Not because it was love at first sight, but because for an instant, he thought she might be Rebecca. When Elena approached, smiling up at him as she asked where she could find Lassen Hall, he'd immediately realized his mistake.

Had he loved her? Certainly not with the single-minded devotion he'd felt as a twenty-year-old for Rebecca.

"What happened between you?" Rebecca asked.

He didn't want to tell her, still felt shame for his part in what had happened to Elena. But he saw coming clean to Rebecca as part of his penance for failing his wife the way he did. "There was a reason Elena seemed fragile. She had…behavior issues. They didn't fully manifest themselves until after Lea was born."

"What kind of issues?"

Regret, sharp-edged, tumbled in his stomach. "Once, in the middle of changing a diaper, she wandered off to do something else, left Lea on the changing table. Another time she sat down to read to Lea when she had supper cooking on the stove. The pan burned and set off the smoke alarm. She was frantic. Luckily a neighbor heard."

The waiter returned with their entrées, taking away the half-eaten egg rolls. Rebecca looked down at her grilled salmon as if she couldn't remember ordering it. He wasn't sure how he'd make his way through the beef Wellington the waiter had brought for him.

Rebecca cut a bite of the tender salmon. "What was wrong with her?"

"A tumor. That was what triggered the aneurism that killed her." A familiar fist of guilt tightened in his chest. "I was ten times an idiot for not seeing the signs sooner. All those months putting in clinic hours at a homeless shelter and I couldn't diagnose my own wife, right under my nose."

"You were a psychologist, not a medical doctor."

"Even still." He shook his head. "I thought she was just irresponsible, that she didn't care about her own daughter. Then one day when Lea was about eighteen months, Elena lay down in the bedroom for a nap. She left Lea playing in the living room with the door wide open. Lea wandered outside, down the sidewalk to the corner. She was about to step into the street when a passerby caught her."

Even now, two-and-a-half years later, he still felt sick at the thought. The woman who had rescued Lea called the police, and it took hours to connect the wandering little girl to him and Elena.

"I couldn't risk Lea's safety anymore. A week later, I filed for divorce. Because of Elena's history with Lea, I got full custody." That day in court, seeing Elena break down, he'd felt like the worst kind of monster.

"When she took her," Rebecca said, "she must have known she might not be able to take good care of her."

"I think Elena thought she could will herself to do better. She didn't know what was going on inside her brain any more than I did."

"But for two years…and she had to have been getting worse."

"From what I understand, from what Darius was able to piece together, Elena had one or two friends who knew to check on Lea. Elena had confided in one woman in particular, asked her to call or come by when she could. I think the woman thought Elena was into drugs. She was the one who found her dead."

So many what-ifs weighed on him. What if he hadn't divorced Elena? He could have hired someone to care for Lea and keep an eye on Elena, as well? Or what if he'd explained more clearly to the au pair about his late wife, made sure she never gave Elena that opportunity to take his daughter? Maybe, somehow, he'd have seen Elena's decline, would have been able to help her.

When he first heard the chiming of a cell phone, he reached reflexively for his waist. When he came up empty, he recalled he'd left his phone on his dresser. By then, Rebecca was retrieving her purse from the floor.

She quickly opened the flip phone. "Hello?" She glanced over at Tony. "Slow down, Kevin, I can't understand what you're saying." Then her eyes went wide. "Did you call 911?"

Panic slammed into Tony. "Who?"

"Estelle," Rebecca said, handing him the phone.

The ambulance was there when Tony pulled into the parking lot, and Rebecca allowed herself a small measure of relief. Kevin had already called back to say Estelle was alert and talking, that the dizziness that had caused her to stumble and fall had passed. But Rebecca wouldn't breathe easy until she saw her former foster mother with her own eyes.

She and Tony ran along the path toward the bunkhouse. The teens were all clustered outside, light spilling from the open door. They had their arms around each other, a couple of the girls wiping away tears.

Ruby held Lea, the little girl's face buried against her shoulder. Ruby must have told Lea her daddy had arrived, because she launched herself from Ruby and pelted toward Tony.

Her thin arms around Tony's neck, Lea sobbed inconsolably, trying to speak, her words broken and incomprehensible. Tony rubbed his daughter's back, murmuring "*Mija, mija,* it's okay" over and over.

His gaze met Ruby's over Lea's head. "What's the matter with Lea?"

"She was there when Grams fell," Ruby told him. "She freaked out when Grams didn't get up right away."

Rebecca exchanged a glance with Tony, sure he ws thinking the same things as she. Lea must have thought what happened to her mother had happened to Estelle."

Rebecca stroked the back of Lea's head. "How's Estelle?" The EMTs had the older woman on the near sofa. The sofa back hid her from view.

Ruby glanced inside the bunkhouse. "Her blood pressure was through the roof—that's why she got dizzy. They've had her lying down for a while, so I think she's doing better."

Kevin edged in closer. "Grams won't go to the hospital."

"Why not?" Rebecca asked.

Kevin shrugged. At Tony's nod, Rebecca stepped inside, stopping behind the sofa out of the way of the two young EMTs. She took in the names on their nametags— Trish and John.

Estelle pushed the oxygen mask from her face. "Heck of a way to get everyone's attention."

Her voice was weak and thready, her complexion sallow. Anxiety all but closed Rebecca's throat.

Rebecca leaned on the back of the sofa and took Estelle's hand. "Why won't you go to the hospital?"

Estelle looked away. "They told me I don't have to."

Trish gave Estelle a disapproving look. "We told her we recommended it. But we can't force her."

"I'm seeing my doctor in a few days," Estelle said. "I'll be fine until then."

Rebecca closed the cold hand in both of hers. "Estelle—"

"Rebecca, please." Estelle's fingers flexed. "Jake went to the hospital. He never came home."

"But you're not dying." As fear flared inside Rebecca, she quickly looked up at the female EMT.

"She's not," Trish said. She tried to put the mask back on Estelle's face, but the older woman held her off.

"I know it's foolish," Estelle said. "Jake had lymphoma and we knew he was near the end. But still, knowing that was the last time he would leave his home…"

Rebecca gently patted Estelle's hand. "We'll all keep an eye on you. If you feel sick…"

"She can call 911," Trish said, positioning the oxygen mask again.

John started packing up his equipment. "She has no symptoms of a stroke. Her blood sugar is normal. She'll have to sign an AMA stating she's refusing transport to the hospital against medical advice, but if she sees her doctor on Tuesday…"

Estelle signed the form they offered her on a clipboard. They checked her blood pressure again, still high but apparently better than before. They left a few minutes later after another reminder to see her doctor.

Tony brought Lea in, the teens waiting their turn. Estelle sat up with Rebecca's help, then let the little girl crawl into her lap.

Lea sobbed, clinging to Estelle. "I thought…you were leaving…like Mama…" She took a shaky breath. "Like Jana."

Chapter Thirteen

As Estelle rubbed Lea's back, Rebecca sat down beside Estelle. "What do you think happened to Jana, sweetheart?"

"She went away," Lea said mournfully.

Tony went down on one knee, eye level with his daughter. "Who told you that, *mija?*"

Lea twisted to face her father. "Jana did, when she came to see me. She read me three stories because she said she wouldn't see me for a while."

Estelle pressed a kiss on the top of Lea's head. "Well, Grams isn't going anywhere. I promise."

The teens came in then, arranging themselves around Estelle, some sitting beside her, a few at her feet, the others draped on the sofa arms and back. They spoke softly, touched her gently, treating her like a piece of delicate crystal.

Tony made the announcement about Jana. There was a moment of openmouthed silence, then Rebecca could see the expressions on some of their faces hardening—Serena and Ari, James and Kevin. This wasn't the first time someone they'd come to care about had walked out of their lives.

Then Ruby rose from the arm of the sofa and took on a businesslike tone. "I'll draw up a schedule on the computer. We'll all sign up for two-hour time slots to take care of Lea. Grams, you'll need to relax for a while, so the rest of us will take over."

"I can't sit around doing nothing," Estelle complained.

"Then answer the phone for me. I can have calls transferred to the house or here." Tony lifted Lea from Estelle's lap and nestled her against his side. "There's some computer work to be done."

"I'll do that," Ruby said.

"Also Jana was developing some more potential donors," Tony said. "With her gone—"

"I can do that, too," Ruby said.

Rebecca stepped forward. "That's too much to take on, Ruby. Besides, I want you and Colleen to help mentor the two new girls who are starting this week. I can make the donor calls."

Katy enthusiastically volunteered for the last piece of Jana's job—keeping the main house tidy. Both Serena and Ari offered to help, and the three decided to rotate through that task just as they would Lea's care.

By the time they'd covered all the details of replacing Jana, Lea was all but nodding off against her father, exhausted by emotions and the long day. *"Mija,"* Tony murmured, "should I take you over to the house?"

Shaking her head, she yawned hugely. "I want to stay here. With Grams."

Colleen pushed to her feet. "I've got her bed all ready." She reached for Lea, transferring the little girl from Tony to herself. She and Lea headed down the hall to the empty bedroom.

Estelle's energy was flagging, as well. Kevin and James helped her up, but she shook off their hands and gestured to Rebecca. "Come walk me to my room."

"I'll wait for you," Tony said.

Rebecca took Estelle's elbow. "Go ahead. I'll be up in a few minutes."

As they passed the boys' old room, Rebecca saw Lea curled up in bed, half-asleep already as Colleen read her a story. She felt a twinge of jealousy at the sight of someone else reading to Tony's daughter. But truly, wasn't that for the best? That Lea could lavish her love on someone other than Rebecca?

Rebecca waited outside Estelle's room while the older woman changed into a nightgown, then went inside when she got the all clear. Estelle lay in bed, the dark circles under her eyes contrasting starkly against her pale skin.

Estelle's larger room provided enough space for a desk and television stand in addition to the double bed and a good-sized dresser. Rebecca recognized a few odds and ends from the Sacramento house—a wedding photo of her and Jake in its worn wood frame, the porcelain mantle clock with its faded pink roses, a mechanical toy bank that had been the pride of Jake's collection. All of Estelle's fosters had been fascinated by that bank, thrilled when Jake would take it off the shelf to show them how the baseball pitcher tossed a coin into the bank's slot.

Arrayed on a shelf above the desk were a collection of crudely made clay figures, the creations of a generation of foster children. Rebecca spotted the one she'd made—a fat turkey with clumsily painted feathers. Her heart ached at the memory of that Thanksgiving without her parents.

She lifted it from the shelf to take a closer look. The fired-on paint was peeling on the turkey's back. "I can't believe you still have this."

"How could I throw it away?" Estelle asked.

Rebecca pulled over the desk chair and sat beside the bed. Estelle's hands, crossed on the bedclothes, looked puffy. "How long have your hands been swollen like this?" Rebecca asked.

Estelle waved off her concern. "It's just the heat. I want to know what's going on with you and Tony."

Flashes of memory tumbled in her mind—Tony touching her, kissing her in the dry stores. "Why would you think anything is going on?"

"I'm not an idiot," she said. "I have eyes."

She would have argued, told Estelle she was seeing something that wasn't there, but why lie? "We're attracted to one another. I guess the years didn't change that."

Estelle's gaze narrowed on her. "There's more to it than attraction. The way you two look at one another—"

"You're mistaken. Tony and I…" She took in a long breath. "There's nothing there for us anymore. I'm not sure if there ever was."

"I don't believe that. Remember, I was there when you first fell in love, there at your wedding. If Alejandro hadn't died—"

"But he did. And what I thought was love, what you thought was love…" She shook her head. "It was a house of cards, Estelle. Two young people so caught up in discovering their bodies they fooled themselves in mistaking sex for love."

"You don't really think that."

"I...I do. Tony does, too." He'd spelled it out at dinner. That if not for her pregnancy, the intense emotions they'd felt for each other would have waned and vanished with time.

Why did that hurt so much? Because a dream she'd always nurtured inside, that she'd once loved Tony, that he'd loved her, had been destroyed? Or because, unlike Tony, she was convinced that her love had been real?

"If I'd loved him, Estelle, how could I have left?"

"Sweetheart." Estelle reached for her hand. "You were in so much pain. Day by day, it only got worse. You weren't eating. You lost so much weight you were like a ghost."

The grief of that time still hunkered inside her, boxed away but always threatening to break loose. "Even still, I shouldn't have left him."

"Because you still loved him?"

What Tony said in the restaurant rolled over again in her mind. "Because it was wrong to leave that way. Because I hurt him so badly, on top of the pain of losing the baby."

"That's all in the past, Becca. What matters is now. What you want now."

Shutting her eyes, she leaned back in her chair. "I want the clarity I had as an eighteen-year-old, the confidence that every decision I made was right."

"Except they weren't always right," Estelle reminded her.

"But I thought they were." She sat up, facing Estelle. "I want to know that I love Tony."

She didn't even realize what she'd said until she saw the surprise on Estelle's face. "That you loved Tony then? Or that you love him now?"

She'd been talking about the past, hadn't she? She didn't love Tony still. She wasn't that confused.

Loving Tony was a losing proposition. He'd spelled it out clearly for her—whatever they'd had in the past wouldn't be rewritten in the present. The feelings they'd once had for each other had been buried even more deeply than memories of their son.

She suddenly felt like weeping. "I'd better let you get some sleep." On her feet, she pecked a kiss on Estelle's cheek. "I'll see you in the morning."

"Becca!" Estelle called after her. But Rebecca hurried out of Estelle's room.

James and Brittany were curled up together on one of the sofas watching television, Ruby and Katy were sprawled on the other, reading magazines. They called out their good-nights as Rebecca passed through, and a rush of affection washed over her. She really liked these kids, would hate to see them leave when they completed the program in December.

She stepped out into the cool night air, moving along the dark path toward the main house. In January, Ruby, Katy, James, Brittany and the others would move on, find jobs and places to live. If Tony kept to his word, found a replacement for her, that person would start over with a new group of students. Of the current residents, only Estelle would still be here, and Lea.

And Tony.

One foot on the bottom porch step, she looked up at the house, the porch light's yellow glow welcoming her. Tony had left at least one downstairs lamp on; she could see its illumination filtering through the curtains. It was nearly eleven; had he already gone up to bed? The thought set off an ache inside her, and only at that moment did she realize how much she had looked forward to seeing him, to being with him alone in the house tonight.

She turned, sinking onto the top porch step. Estelle had asked what it was she wanted now. Her answer had been honest enough, but it hadn't been complete. She didn't just want the clarity of youth. She wanted to feel that way again. She wanted to again feel the love she'd once felt.

Except… She looked back over her shoulder, longing throbbing in her body like a live thing. Except she did feel that love. Just as powerfully, just as real as what she'd felt at eighteen. A mother's love for Lea that she'd never been able to lavish on her own son. And a woman's love for Tony.

She loved him. Maybe she had never stopped. Or maybe she had finally matured enough to grow into it. It had been too big for her once to get her arms around it, to fully absorb its magnitude. But now, thirty years old, a son buried, a second marriage come and gone, what had once eluded her, had been too painful to bear, shone in her heart like a brilliant candle.

Except this time, the flame would never burn out. A hurricane couldn't extinguish that spark, a flood couldn't douse it.

She loved Tony. Except it was too late.

On the sofa, the *Mountain Democrat* in his lap, Tony heard her footfalls on the porch steps. There had been no point in going up to his room until he knew she was home. He'd had the foolish notion that he could concentrate enough on the newspaper to catch up on the local news.

When she lingered outside, he grew even edgier, wanting her inside, wondering if there was anything wrong. He'd just pushed to his feet, tossing aside the *Democrat*, when he heard her cross the porch. By the time she opened the door, he was there, just on the other side.

He pulled her toward him, folding her in his arms and bending down to kiss her in one motion. Her mouth against his felt like coming home, the missing piece to the puzzle finally falling into place. She tasted familiar and exotic all at once, the untested girl and the mature, sexual being that was Rebecca now.

Her silk blouse felt tissue-paper thin under his hands, the heat of her body easily breaching that frail barrier. Her breasts pressed against his chest, tantalizing and torturing him with their warm softness.

Her hand drifted down along his side, setting off tremors in his belly. Then she moved lower. When she spread her fingers across the placket of his slacks, pressing against the fullness there, he nearly went to his knees.

He drew his mouth away from hers and trailed kisses along her jaw. "I want you so badly. But you have to know, I can't make promises."

"I don't need promises," she whispered.

Something in her voice made the words ring false, but then her fingers closed around him again, driving sense from his brain. All that mattered was getting her upstairs and into his bed, lying naked in his arms.

He took her hand and led her across the living room, pausing to kiss her, slip his tongue inside her mouth for another taste. On the stairs he kissed her twice, again on the landing, once more as he moved across the threshold to his bedroom. She tasted sweeter each time, her mouth softer, delicious with warmth.

He wanted to tear off her blouse, strip her skirt from her hips. It had been a long time since he'd lain with a woman, and this was his Becca, the focus of so many fantasies, the answer to every question asked in the dark of night. But at the same time he wanted to linger over every touch, savor every cry of pleasure from her lips.

He sat on the edge of the bed, wedging her between his legs. His hands shaking, he slipped free the buttons of her blouse, opening it wider with each one. When he reached the waistband of her skirt, he tugged the blouse from it slowly, the tickle of silk against his palms not nearly as satiny as the feel of Becca's skin.

Loosing the last two buttons, he parted her blouse, letting it drop from her shoulders. The raspberry-pink silk puddled against her crooked arms, the freckled skin of her shoulders intriguing, arousing. She wore a simple white bra, but somehow its plain practicality was more erotic than the most lacy confection would have been.

As his thumbs hooked under the straps, he lifted his gaze to hers. Was there doubt there? The beginnings of regret? Straps still in place, he cupped his hands around her shoulders.

"Are you sure?" he asked, then prayed she wouldn't say no.

She bent to kiss him, soft, lingering, her lips moist against his. "I'm sure."

He drew the straps from her shoulders, baring them completely. Then he reached behind her to release the hooks. She shifted her arms and both the blouse and bra fell to the floor.

Damn, he'd forgotten how beautiful, how lush her breasts were. As a girl, she'd been embarrassed by their size, by the way some men would leer at her. He'd decked one of the boys at Estelle's when the kid had made a crack about Becca.

His hands itched to cup them, to test their weight, their fullness. Instead, he let his hands drift down her arms, to her waist. Tugging on the skirt's elastic band, he let it slide past her hips, then to the floor. She stepped free of the skirt then pushed her pantyhose down to her hips. He took them the rest of the way, letting his fingers trail along her thighs, stroking the backs of her knees, her calves. He took his time unstrapping her sandals, stroking her ankles, the curve of her arch.

Her panties matched the bra, plain cotton knit that nevertheless drove him wild as he contemplated what lay beneath. There was a faint shadow at the vee of her legs beneath the pristine white. The feel of the crisp curls still lingered against his palm, a flashback of when he'd touched her that day in the dry stores.

He kissed her there, inhaling her scent. Her breath caught; her hands gripped his shoulders. His dress shirt seemed too restrictive, and he wanted to tear it from his body. Dragging in a lungful of air, he unfastened his cuffs, then pulled the buttoned shirt up over his head. Easing Rebecca back, he rose and rid himself of his slacks and shorts just as quickly.

His erection pressed against her, the feel of that plain cotton knit exquisite torture. He dipped his hand inside, felt the dampness between her legs. He was tempted to bring her to climax the same way he'd done before, but she grabbed his wrist and with a look of faint annoyance, pulled his hand free.

"It's my turn," she said.

Skimming off her panties, she pushed him back to the edge of the bed. Dropping to her knees, she spread his legs, then wrapped her fingers around him. In the next moment, she had her mouth on him and he thought his heart would explode from his chest.

Her tongue moved against him, wetting the head, burning a trail along the hard length. Her hand cupped the soft sac at the base, the sensations emptying the breath from his lungs. His heart beat in his ears so loudly, he thought he would shake apart.

"Enough," he groaned, lifting her head. "I want to come inside you."

He pulled her to her feet, urged her onto the bed. While she tugged back the covers, he found the condoms he'd bought a week ago and stowed in the drawer of his nightstand. He'd had no idea he'd get this far with her, but he was damn well going to be prepared.

Protection in place, he joined her on the bed, settling in the cradle of her thighs. For a moment, despite the intense sensations, the paradise waiting for him, the memories crowded back, blinding him to the present. This was Becca in his bed, the girl who had burrowed so deeply into his heart, he thought he would love her forever.

He shook off the past with the first plunge inside her. Then he could think of nothing, only feel, only lose himself to pleasure. Slickness and heat, soft sighs and tantalizing scents. The luscious taste of her mouth. Heaven opened up in his arms.

Her cries grew louder as she drew closer to the edge

with each thrust. He wanted perfection for her, ecstasy that would drive her beyond reason. As her ankles locked at the small of his back, bringing him deeper inside her, he felt her tremble as tension grew. He remembered this, the way Becca felt as climax neared, as she lost control.

Then she dropped over the precipice and flew, moaning, her head thrown back, her thighs tightening around his hips. Her body clenched around his as he thrust a last time before climaxing himself. Every nerve ending exploded as he groaned, long and low, against her neck.

He lay there, stunned, with only enough presence of mind to support himself on his elbows to keep his full weight off her. His face buried in the curve of her neck and shoulder, he pressed a kiss on the sweat-dewed skin. She tasted of salt and Becca.

He didn't want to move. He could have lain there for the rest of his life. Made love to her a million more times. But practicality intruded. With a last kiss he pulled away, padded into the bathroom to clean up.

When he returned, she'd pulled the sheet up to her chin and her gaze was wary. Passion still colored her cheeks, the wash of pink stirring him again as he approached the bed.

He stood over her, trying to decipher the message in those soft brown eyes, to decode the jumble of emotions he felt himself. They probably ought to talk about what they'd done. She'd likely want to know what it meant and didn't mean. But he had no answers for her. At least not tonight.

So he pulled back the sheet and climbed in beside her. Switched off the light beside the bed. He nestled her body against his, pillowing her shoulders with his arm.

Right now, he could pretend that tomorrow didn't

matter. He could blank the past from his mind, wipe away all the old sins, real or imagined. Just hold Becca, breathe in her scent.

Pretend he had forever.

Chapter Fourteen

When Tony woke at seven Sunday morning, Rebecca was gone. In those first drowsy moments, panic hit him—she'd gone for good, had left him once again. Then the sound of the shower registered and he forced the crazy fear aside.

If she hadn't been downstairs in her own bathroom, he would have slipped into the shower with her, made love to her again under the warm, wet spray. He still could. If he hurried downstairs before she finished, he could catch her before she dried off and dressed.

As he pushed himself upright, about to toss aside the sheet, he spotted his daughter in the doorway. Yanking up the covers, he smiled at Lea. "Hey, *mija*. When did you get home?"

She trotted toward the bed. "Katy brought me cuz I was hungry."

"How'd you get in?"

"Becca. We knocked and she opened the door."

Still wearing her clothes from last night? He didn't want to think about what Katy might make of that.

Something on the floor caught Lea's attention. "How come you gots Becca's shoe?"

He leaned over the edge of the bed. One of Rebecca's sandals poked halfway out from underneath. It must have been hidden by the covers, exposed just now when he'd pulled them up.

At a loss for an answer appropriate for a four-year-old, he avoided the question. "Go change, *mija*. I'll get you something to eat."

Once she was out of sight, he got up and shut his bedroom door. So much for surprising Rebecca in the shower. So much for discretion if she was still wearing that raspberry silk blouse and filmy skirt of hers. Katy might find math challenging, but she could put two and two together.

By the time he'd showered and dressed for eight o'clock mass, Rebecca and Lea were at the breakfast table, his daughter shoveling in Froot Loops and Rebecca nibbling on toast. She wore her usual uniform of short-sleeved white blouse and black slacks, her hair skimmed back in a snug ponytail.

She might as well be wearing a skimpy teddy instead of her prim working gear. He reacted the same, aroused just by the sight of her.

"Did you want to come to mass with me?" The question seemed entirely at odds with the images dancing in his mind.

She shook her head. "We still have a fair amount of prep for our ten o'clock opening."

Today they'd start at ten and close at three. Sam had

promised the students a movie and dinner after they'd finished cleanup this afternoon.

"Who's lined up to watch Lea this morning?"

"She'll be in the kitchen with me until ten, when it gets too busy. Then Ruby's on duty for the next couple hours."

He'd have to post an ad for the assistant position soon. It wasn't fair to ask the students to babysit his daughter.

On the heels of that thought, he remembered Helen Franks. The woman who might well take Rebecca's place. He should tell her. They should talk about it.

Except if they did, it would make it more real, more possible. Make it that much easier for Rebecca to leave. Which was what he'd intended when he hired her. And yet…

Putting on blinders against the future, he shifted gears. "You answered the door when Katy brought Lea home."

"I was about to get in the shower."

"So you were wearing…"

"My robe. I'd just changed out of my—" she glanced over at Lea "—pajamas."

Even as relief shot through him, memories from last night tumbled in his mind. Damn, he wanted to kiss her. If not for his wide-eyed, all-too-observant daughter, he would have.

And Rebecca knew it. He could see the heat in her gaze. The way her lips parted, the way her breath seemed to catch.

"You might want to ask Lea about your shoe," he said softly. Color crept into Rebecca's cheeks, tempting him all the more to touch her. Resolutely, he turned away, heading for the door.

Outside, the coolness of the early morning air dissipated some of the heat clinging to his skin. But it would have taken a blizzard to wipe the X-rated fantasies completely from his mind.

A good long time after Tony left, Rebecca was still struggling to get her bearings. Last night had all but knocked her world completely off its foundations. A part of her wanted to run away as fast as she could, another part to fling herself toward disaster.

Which loving Tony would be. He'd made it clear so many times, in so many ways, that he had no intention of trying to recreate the past. For Tony, sex was one thing, love an entirely different matter. He'd been expert in bed, had brought her exquisite pleasure. But he'd given her no sign that it had been more to him than physical release.

Yet she loved him. Every kiss, every touch, her love for him had spilled silently from her heart. It had clamored so loudly within her, it surprised her he didn't hear, didn't sense. It had taken everything in her not to shout out the truth of it when she'd climaxed.

As she and Lea walked along the path to the bakeshop, they met up with Estelle. The night's rest seemed to have done her some good. The shadows under the older woman's eyes had diminished.

Estelle gave Lea the key to the bakeshop and sent the little girl on ahead. She slowed her steps, forcing Rebecca to slow as well.

"Did you find any answers?" Estelle asked.

For a moment, Rebecca stood there thunderstruck. How could Estelle have known what turbulent thoughts were whirling in Rebecca's mind?

But of course she couldn't know. She was only picking up the thread of their conversation from the night before. She smiled, tried to instill a lightness in her tone. "No great revelations."

Estelle stopped her, still a few yards from Lea who had just managed to wiggle the key into the lock. "The two of you need to figure out what it is you really want."

"There's nothing to figure out, Estelle." She took a step toward the door.

"He's interviewing your replacement."

Rebecca turned back, a knot tightening in her stomach. "How do you know?"

"He mentioned receiving her résumé a few days ago. On Friday, he had his office window open and I heard part of the phone call when he spoke with her."

And Tony hadn't said a word. Had made love to her last night, performed the most intimate acts with her, yet never mentioned the woman who might take her place here.

She struggled to pull herself together. Through the trees beyond the cottage, Rebecca could see Katy making her way over to the bakeshop. The rest of them would be arriving soon.

She shrugged, as if what Estelle had told her was a trivial matter. "When I started here, I only committed to the first session. Tony told me he'd look for someone else to take my place. I just didn't know he'd found someone."

Lea had gotten the door open and now waited for them to follow her inside. Katy drew nearer. "Everyone else is on their way," she called out. "I'm only here on time because sweetpea got me up so early."

They went inside, Rebecca starting a pot of coffee while Estelle took Lea out to the dining room to gather the salt and pepper shakers on a tray. Katy went to check on the day's stock of coffee cake, turnovers and peach cobbler.

James and Brittany wandered in first, all but glued together. Ruby and Serena drifted in several minutes later, Ari a few minutes after them. Colleen and Kevin were conspicuous by their absence.

Rebecca saw the looks exchanged by Ruby and Katy and had an uneasy suspicion of what Kevin and Colleen might be up to. When they finally turned up fifteen minutes later, the girl's dark hair mussed, Kevin's shirt buttoned wrong, Rebecca's hunch was confirmed.

She took them each by the arm and marched them to the back of the kitchen, out of earshot of the others. "Kevin, fix your shirt."

He flushed beet red. His fingers fumbled with the buttons. "Didn't notice."

"You two are late. And it's not the first time, either." Rebecca cut to the chase. "Are you two using protection?"

Now Colleen's cheeks matched Kevin's. "That's none of your business."

"The hell it isn't." One more quarter for the cuss jar, but it was for a good cause. "How do you think it'll look for Tony and Estelle's House if a student from his first session turns up pregnant?"

Guilt flickered in Kevin's eyes. "She's not pregnant."

"For how long?" Rebecca asked. "Careless people end up with unexpected consequences. Believe me, a baby will turn your world upside down."

Colleen's expression turned mulish. "Maybe I want a baby."

Kevin's eyes all but popped from his head. "Colleen!"

"You don't. Not now." Rebecca put one hand on each

of their shoulders, bringing them in close. "I know a little bit about it. I got pregnant at eighteen."

"But you and Tony were married," Colleen said.

"Not until after I found out. And it was hard being married so young. Harder than you can imagine."

Colleen lowered her voice to a whisper. "What happened to the baby?"

So few people knew she'd had a child—Tony, Estelle, Sam. She'd never even shared the painful secret with Phillip. Revealing the truth to Colleen and Kevin likely meant opening that circle even wider when they passed on what they'd learned to the others.

But maybe it was time to shine a light on the past. "He was stillborn. A genetic defect."

They both stared at her a long time before Kevin said softly, "I'll make sure she's protected."

Rebecca nodded, then returned to the work area, where her crew all seemed to have one ear on the drama that had just unfolded. She doubted they'd heard anything, but if past experience was any guide they would all know what had transpired between the three of them within the hour.

When Tony stepped into the kitchen at a quarter to ten, eight pairs of eyes fixed on him with avid curiosity. They followed him as he pulled a clean folded apron from the shelf and tied it on, finally looking away as he grabbed a hairnet and popped it over his hair.

Rebecca seemed to be the only one focused on her work, arranging frozen apple turnovers on a metal tray. Tugging on a pair of latex gloves, he took up a post beside her to help. "What did I miss?" he asked.

All eight teens seemed to make an effort to keep their

backs to him and Rebecca. She pitched her voice low. "They know about Alejandro." She proceeded to fill him in on Colleen and Kevin's shenanigans as well as the lecture she'd given them.

"It's not as if I didn't expect something like this to come up with a coed program. They're all eighteen, legal adults."

"So were we."

He could hear the rest of her unspoken thought. *Look how that turned out.*

"Are you okay with all of them knowing?" he asked.

"Why shouldn't they?" She took a shaky breath. "There was no reason to hide our marriage. They should know about him, too."

He suddenly realized her control was razor-thin. Blocking her from view, he turned her toward the privacy of the dry stores. Once out of eyesight of the others, he pulled her into his arms. She buried her face against his chest, her fingers digging into his sides as she fought the tears.

"All these years, I thought it would hurt less if I never thought about him. If I never remembered the pregnancy, all the hopes we had for him. If I never visited his grave, the pain would go away more quickly." She drew a sobbing breath. "How stupid could I be?"

Tony stroked her back, wishing he could draw the hurt away. But after his brief counsel this morning with Father Joseph, he knew she'd have to find her own path to forgiveness.

A path he was still following. "I felt the same way at first, Becca. That forgetting him would be best. But he never let me. Even though he never opened his eyes.

Never—" the pain swamped him "—never smiled at me. He was still so real, I couldn't pretend he never existed."

The rising noise level in the kitchen and dining room signaled them that opening time had arrived. He released Rebecca, following her into the kitchen. As she splashed water on her face at the sink, the teens seemed to make it a point to look the other way.

Ruby and Estelle hustled Lea off to the bunkhouse as the dining room quickly filled with customers. The kids' fifteen seconds of fame on last night's local news had spread word of their enterprise much farther afield than Tony could have hoped for in his wildest dreams.

They ran out of their Sunday stock before noon. By one, Rebecca called over to ask Ruby to make up a sign on the computer announcing that the Estelle's House bakeshop would have to curtail their Monday hours. By two-thirty, the sign was altered to regretfully state that the Monday menu would be limited due to unexpected demand on Sunday.

Constantly in motion, Rebecca seemed determined to distract herself from her earlier grief. Maybe she figured if she kept moving, she could outrun the tears she'd spilled in the dry stores room. She had run away from him, she had run away from the loss of Alejandro. Maybe it was the only way she knew to cope with the unbearable.

As he collected dirty dishes and trash from a just-vacated table, he reflected on what Father Joseph had told him. That his forgiving Rebecca for leaving wasn't for her benefit, but for his. As long as he kept a death grip on his anger, his sense of betrayal, he would never heal from that decade-old tragedy. All these years he'd kept Alejandro linked with Rebecca's abandonment of their marriage. He had to separate the two, find a way to forgive her for what had once seemed unforgivable.

He was beginning to think he could forgive. But seeing Rebecca now, the way she dashed from task to task as if the devil were in pursuit, he wondered if his absolution would even matter to her. She was like a bird perched on a tree branch, flitting away from the least peril. Except in Rebecca's case, it wasn't fear that sent her flying: it was grief.

Sam showed up at three just as the last of the crowd filtered out the door. The teens flowed toward him like water spilling over a dam, eager to share their excitement over the day's success. He gave the girls hugs and slapped the boys on the back as he made his way toward the kitchen where Tony stood in the doorway.

Rebecca had finally settled, sitting at one of the tables with her feet up in a chair. A towel in his hands, Tony gripped and twisted the damp terry cloth to give himself something to do besides walk over there and touch her. He wanted to set her feet in his lap and rub them as he had yesterday. Then he wanted to take her up to the house and do some of the other things they'd done the day before.

Sam must have seen something in Tony's face. He wagged one brow, all but leering. "You two are getting along, I take it."

"I don't know what we're doing." He turned on his heel to retreat to the kitchen, tossing the towel on the center island. "You're taking the kids to the movies?"

"You planning on coming with us?"

"Is Rebecca going?"

"The kids were going to try to talk her into it," Sam said. Through the service window, he saw Brittany in animated conversation with Rebecca. Rebecca shrugged, then nodded. Apparently, she'd said yes.

"I think I'd better stay here," he told Sam. Even with the teens around, he didn't think sitting in a dark theater with Rebecca was such a great idea.

"Mind if I borrow the Suburban? The DeLorean would be a tight squeeze."

"Sure." He dug in his pocket for his key ring, took off the SUV's key and handed it over.

Sam flipped the key end-over-end across his fingers, a throwback to the sleight of hand he'd practiced as a boy. "Other than Oregon, did Jana say where she was going?"

"No forwarding address, if that's what you mean."

"What about her cell?"

"Why the sudden interest in Jana?" Tony asked.

Sam, a master at hiding a multitude of secrets behind those blue eyes, didn't answer. He just waited, the key in constant motion.

Tony knew he wasn't likely to get a response. "If she took her cell with her, she's not answering it. I can give you the number if you'd like to try."

"Already have it. She's not taking calls, either." He dropped the key in his pocket and strode out to the dining room. "Let's get in gear, folks," he called out. "We have a movie to go to."

With that motivation, the teens accomplished cleanup in record time. But even working at speed, they weren't sloppy. The boys made sure they swept and mopped every crumb, the girls took great care in packing away leftovers and scrubbing every surface until it sparkled. They were competent and confident.

At the start of the program, they'd constantly looked to

Rebecca for direction, for confirmation that they'd accomplished a task correctly. But thanks to Rebecca's high expectations for them, they now had the self-assurance to do the work themselves without needing her constant supervision.

Tony thought about Helen, the woman he'd spoken with on Friday, wondered how well she'd interact with this team. Helen had e-mailed him yesterday morning to let him know which days in the upcoming week she could come for an in-person interview. He hadn't replied yet, wasn't even sure why he was waffling.

The kitchen emptied as the teens headed over to the bunkhouse and cottage to change. He hadn't seen Rebecca leave; only Estelle and Lea were still out in the dining room.

"So, what's it gonna be, *mija?*" he asked his daughter. "Go to the movies with Grams or stay home with the old man?"

"I want to go with Grams."

Tony glanced up at Estelle. "Will it work having her along?"

She nodded. "We're splitting up at the theater. Lea and I are checking out that new kids' movie. The rest of the group are still trying to decide between the action film or the horror flick."

Tony guessed that Rebecca would join Estelle and Lea at the kids' film. He bent to give his daughter a hug. "Have a good time, *mija*. Don't eat too much popcorn."

Lea dashed out the dining room's back door, Estelle following more slowly. After they'd gone, he hung back, reluctant to head over to the empty house. Maybe he should have agreed to go with them after all. He could have ridden over in his Suburban while Rebecca drove her car, could watch the action movie with the teens instead of the animated film Lea would be going to with Estelle and Rebecca.

Except when he did a mental count, he realized they'd need a third car if he went with them. No doubt they already had the seating set in the Suburban and Rebecca's Corolla. There was no room for him to squeeze in.

Damned if he didn't feel left out. In the years he lived with Estelle, she always did her best to include her fosters in extracurricular activities if she and Jake could scrape together the extra funds. Often enough, though, she and Jake just wouldn't have the wherewithal and Tony would have to tell his friends he couldn't go on the camping trip or to the ball game.

He reminded himself he'd chosen not to go tonight and shook off the pang of loneliness. Wandering into the kitchen, he dug a couple of boneless chicken breasts from the freezer, then tracked down a fat red bell pepper and onion in the walk-in. He had a few flour tortillas in his fridge. His repertoire might not be as extensive as Rebecca's, but he could make pretty mean fajitas.

His groceries in a plastic market bag, he made his way to the house. Along the way he crossed paths with Katy, Ruby, Serena and Ari heading toward the cars. Sam was leaning up against the Suburban talking to Kevin and James. Rebecca's car was sandwiched between the Suburban and the DeLorean. With the afternoon glare on the windshield, he couldn't see if she was already inside.

He waved from the porch as they piled into the vehicles. Rebecca's Corolla backed out, then pulled in behind the Suburban. With the sun's copper glare, he couldn't make out her face in the driver's seat, didn't know if she'd waved back at him. In spite of himself, he felt a little like that boy watching his friends drive off to a Giants game in San Francisco that he would have given his left arm to be able to attend.

He took the bag to the kitchen, setting the frozen breasts on a plate to defrost and putting the veggies in the fridge. There were still a couple hours before he'd want dinner. The time yawned before him, and he was at a loss as to how to fill it.

Just as he started toward the living room where he'd left a paperback he'd been reading, he heard footsteps from the direction of the downstairs bedroom. As he wondered who the hell was in the house, the faint scent of lilacs drifted toward him. Seconds later, Rebecca emerged, her hair wrapped in a towel, a skimpy robe tied around her waist.

Chapter Fifteen

Her heart pounding, Rebecca stared at Tony. "I thought you left for the movies."

He took a step toward her. "Sam said you were going. I saw you say yes to Brittany."

"She asked if they could borrow my car."

Another step closer. "Why did you stay?"

"After last night—" she couldn't suppress a shiver "—I needed some space. Some time alone to think."

Now he stood over her, so near she could feel his heat. "I could go," he said in a near whisper. "Upstairs, or out to my office. Leave you by yourself."

She shook her head, leaning toward him, helpless to walk away. He loosed the towel on her head, letting it drop to the floor. With his fingers he combed the tangles from her wet hair until it fell around her shoulders.

He traced the shape of her ear with a fingertip. "I've got a feeling we've been set up."

A shudder ran through her. "By who?"

"Sam. Estelle. They knew we'd be left behind together."

He reached for the tie to her robe, loosening the knot. The satin robe fell open. He drew his hand along the opening, from her collarbone, down between her breasts, then lower. He spread his fingers over her belly, his thumb just brushing her navel, his pinkie just above the curls at the vee of her legs.

"How many times did we make love before you got pregnant? Twice? Three times?"

His palm started slow circles against her. "It was the third time," she gasped.

She felt his laugh rather than heard it. "The fourth time I finally used a condom. Too late."

As he continued to stroke, he lowered his mouth to hers. His tongue dove inside, thrusting in rhythm with his touch. His erection pressed against her thigh each time his fingers dipped low.

He trailed kisses across her cheek to her ear. "Your body changed so quickly. Your breasts—" he brought his other hand up to cup the heavy weight "—got even bigger." He laughed again. "Talk about an adolescent fantasy."

He teased her nipple between his fingers, sending a shot of sensation between her thighs. Her knees grew weak as she struggled to keep her feet.

His hands still on her, he moved backward, urging her toward the sofa. Lowering himself, he pulled her down on top of him. She straddled him, the robe slithering off her shoulders, down her arms and off. Her hair felt damp and cool against the back of her neck, an enticing contrast to the heat of his touch.

"Your body has changed again." He spanned her waist with his hands. "More curves. Your breasts are even more luscious."

He pulled her down, bringing a nipple into his mouth. As he sucked and scraped the sensitive flesh lightly with his teeth, a honeyed warmth pooled between her thighs.

"The condoms are upstairs," he rasped out.

She tensed to get to her feet, but he didn't let go. "Move up," he whispered. "I want to taste you."

Mesmerized by the low rumble of his voice, she repositioned her body near his shoulders. He eased himself lower until his mouth was at the juncture of her thighs.

She cried out at the first touch of his tongue between her folds, her fingers digging into the back of the sofa. He drew circles again, smaller, more intense. Each arc of his tongue pushed her higher toward cataclysm, drove moans of pleasure from her throat.

When he plunged his fingers inside her, she closed around him in convulsive release, feeling herself explode in a million different pieces. Another touch of his tongue and she came again, throwing back her head as she called out his name.

As she trembled, loose-limbed, too sated to stay upright, he shifted her until she lay full-length against him. Lying naked against his fully dressed body seemed incredibly erotic. The feel of his clothes against her skin aroused her all over again.

"I want you in my bed," he murmured in her ear.

He helped her up, lifting her naked body in his arms. He carried her up the stairs, into his room. The covers were still rumpled, the sheets still scented with the musk of sex.

As she lay back on the bed, he undressed quickly, his

hot dark gaze fixed on her. He sheathed himself with protection, then stretched out beside her. Pulling her on top of him, he spread her legs.

"Take me inside you."

There was no way she could deny him. Her heart all but burst with love for him, so overwhelming she was certain he could see the truth in her face.

He kept his gaze locked with hers as she lowered herself onto him, his eyes fluttering closed as she took him fully inside. He pushed up with his hips, filling her then drawing back. Her body still sensitized by its earlier pleasure, she was brought quickly back to the brink. Sensing how closely she balanced on the edge, he plunged inside her, hands gripping her hips, holding himself pressed against her.

Her orgasm rolled over her, flinging her from reality into an exquisite paradise. As she cried out, she felt his release, his groan torn from him. Her world centered on the physical connection between them, on the emotional link between her heart and his.

The words *I love you* rang in her ears and she realized with a shock that she'd said them out loud. Her gaze dropped to his face, still tight in the aftermath of passion Maybe he hadn't heard. Maybe he'd been so caught up in climax her slip didn't register with him.

But then his eyes drifted open, zeroed in on her. With the window blinds partly shut, sunshine slanted across his face, stripes of light and shadow. It was difficult to parse his expression, to ferret out his reaction to what she'd said.

He reached for her, bringing her down to brush a kiss across her mouth. Then he eased out from under her, rolling from the bed. As he disappeared into the bathroom, shutting the door behind him, she tried to put the pieces of the puzzle together. Was he angry with her for spilling out her secret? Or did he just feel nothing, not caring one way or another?

When he returned to the bedroom, he tugged on his shorts again, then a pair of jeans he dug from a dresser drawer. He handed over a T-shirt. She pulled it on, grateful for a chance to cover herself.

As she brought her knees to her chest, tucking them under the too-large T-shirt, he sat on the edge of the bed. She wanted him next to her, his arms around her, not at the foot of the bed out of reach.

He laced then unlaced his fingers in his lap. Finally he looked at her. "This isn't how I wanted it to go," he said quietly.

She wrapped her arms around her shins. "What did you want?" she forced herself to ask.

He shrugged. "That we could make love without…"

"Without me loving you?"

She saw the agony in his face. "I can't let myself believe, Becca. I did that once. You ripped out my heart. Your leaving just about killed me."

Shame engulfed her. "I don't deserve a second chance."

"It's not about what you deserve or what I deserve. There's someone else in the picture now. Lea. I have to be strong for her. If you pull the world out from under me again, if I go through what I went through before…"

Tears brimmed in her eyes. "I love your daughter." Her heart ached with that love.

"I have to put her first." His voice was rough with emotion. "This—" he gestured at the bed "—was a mistake. I think we both know that. But being close to you every day, having you back in my life... I let myself pretend." He shook his head. "But I just can't revisit the past."

They sat in the heavy silence of the room, Tony's shoulders sagging. He stared down at his hands as if they somehow held the answers to untangling the knot of their problems. Rebecca wanted nothing more than to close the distance between them, lay her arm around him. Press her cheek against his shoulder.

She loved him so powerfully. But the way she'd hurt him before, how did she know that same weakness, that same cowardice, wouldn't defeat her again? That the love that should be a rock wouldn't turn into a weapon against her? She wanted to believe she was strong enough to stand against an unguessable future and the pain and grief it might hold. But could she risk the damage she might do to Tony and Lea if she crumbled?

Agony gripping her like a live thing, she slid from the bed. The T-shirt fell to her hips; she wished it covered her from head to toe. She desperately wanted to run, to hide.

She forced herself to face him. "Estelle tells me you've been interviewing a woman to be my replacement."

His gaze lifted to meet hers. "Helen looks good on paper, sounded okay over the telephone, but I haven't met her yet."

"When is she coming out to the ranch?"

"I told her Thursday. Give the two new girls a couple days to settle in."

"If she works out, if the teens respond well to her—" she crossed her arms over her middle, trying to hold the pain at bay "—I'm thinking I should leave earlier than we agreed. We could have a few weeks of overlap, then Helen could take over."

Anger flared in his eyes, then a moment later it was as if a veil dropped over his face. As if she'd done exactly what he'd expected her to do. But wasn't it better to do it now than make promises she couldn't be certain she would be capable of keeping?

"I'd have to check with Helen, see if she could get out of her contract early." His mouth set in a hard line. "If so, I'm glad to release you from our agreement. If Lea knows in advance you're leaving, I think she can handle it. She did with Jana."

"That's good," she said, although it felt anything but in the pit of her stomach. It took everything in her to stand there, to finish. "We can't do this again. We can't take this any further than we already have."

He stared at her, long moments beating away. "I won't touch you."

The four simple words of his vow felt like body blows. With a tip of her head in acknowledgment, she walked from the room. She gripped the handrail on the stairs to keep from collapsing as she descended, then tightened her hands into fists for the short walk across to her bedroom. The moment she stepped inside, she raced to the bathroom, overcome by nausea.

Once her stomach was empty, she collapsed on the cold tile floor, wrenched by sobs. She was nineteen years old again, struck with the freight train of grief with the death of her son. Just as she couldn't bring him back to life then, she couldn't change Tony's bone deep belief that she would again abandon him.

How could she convince him to believe in her when she didn't believe in herself?

* * *

Tony went through the motions of making dinner, taking no pleasure in the process of sautéing peppers, onions and chicken, heating the tortillas, grating the cheese. When he finished the fajitas, he set two plates at the kitchen table, then knocked on Rebecca's door, calling out, "Dinner's ready" before walking away. He hadn't seen her in the two hours since she left his room. He doubted she'd join him for dinner.

So he sat at the table alone, eating mechanically when he had no appetite. He didn't even hear her stir. For all he knew, she was asleep, the anguish he'd seen in her eyes extinguished by oblivion.

He could do with some oblivion himself. He considered the six-pack in the back of his fridge, the chilled bottles a perfect accompaniment both to his meal and his emotional turmoil. All six of them might do the trick, at least for tonight. But he had no appetite for beer, either.

He rinsed his dishes, stowed them in the dishwasher. Put away the leftovers. Knocked again on Rebecca's door to say, "Fajitas are in the fridge if you want them."

About to go upstairs to his own room, he made a detour into the living room. Her robe was still there. It had slithered to the floor beside the sofa when he'd urged her up to his mouth. The memories of the taste of her, her feminine musk, set off heat inside him. The images made him hard, goaded him to go to her door and knock again.

He picked up her robe, held it to his face. Breathed in the fragrance of her shampoo. He let himself be inundated with fragments of his life with her—the years at Estelle's, their first kiss, the first time they made love. The joys of their marriage, the searing tragedy of Alejandro's death. All of it precious, irreplaceable. Just as she was.

Yet she was going. Maybe in as little as a few weeks. She gave him fair warning this time. He would have time to prepare.

The robe in his hands, he climbed the stairs. Went into his room and shut the door. Kicked off his shoes and stretched out on the bed.

As he lay there, staring up at the ceiling, the satin robe in a rumpled pile beside him, he realized it was time to face the truth. He loved her. Whether it was newly born since she'd returned into his life or had never died, he loved her. Elena had just been a hope for a new beginning, a hope that had never borne fruit. Because his heart had never ended its commitment to Rebecca.

Why not let himself love her? Why not go downstairs now, confess to her? He could take whatever time they might have together, close his mind to the prospect of her leaving. There were no guarantees in life—look what happened to Alejandro. To Elena.

But Lea didn't understand that. If he married Rebecca, then she left him like she did before, it would add yet another stone to his daughter's heart. He couldn't protect Lea from everything, but he could shield her from the more likely hurts.

Because Rebecca had made no promises when she'd declared she loved him. Had put up no defense when he'd told her he couldn't take a chance on her. As if she didn't trust her own self to do the right thing.

If she didn't trust herself, how could he?

Chapter Sixteen

She felt hollowed out, as if all emotion had been blanched from her. The only thing left inside was an unrelenting pain.

Yet as the days dragged on after her conversation with Tony, she would return again and again to the realization that she'd made the right decision. Leaving here, cutting all ties, was the only answer, the only way to protect Lea.

Monday they sold out by noon, and the teens were giddy with joy. When Tony toted up the weekend's receipts, put aside the costs they'd calculated ahead of time and reserves for the program going forward, there was still a tidy sum to be divided amongst the eight students.

Tony and Sam had been determined that each partici-pant would have a nest egg when they completed the program. The money acted as both an incentive to retain the students for the entire five months and as a leg up for them when they went out on their own.

On Tuesday, they finally got the word from Estelle's doctor. As the EMTs had already told her, her blood pressure was far higher than it should be, but Dr. Patel seemed confident Estelle would be able to control it with an ACE inhibitor and a diuretic. When she returned to the ranch with a relieved smile and a bottle of medication, the teens swarmed her, hugging her and all but carrying her to the bunkhouse.

That afternoon, the two new students, Shawna and Maria, arrived. The two girls were both quiet and withdrawn and went to their room in the bunkhouse with scarcely a hello to the others.

After they'd gone, Tony called Rebecca into his office. Rebecca had managed to avoid being alone with him the past two days and would have begged off today. But she knew how important it was that they discuss the new arrivals.

She sat in the worn office chair, opposite Tony behind his desk. "How much do you know about them?" she asked.

"They've been through some tough times."

"Worse than the others?"

"Much worse." Tony glanced over at the file on his desk. "Once they start coming out of their shells, some of that old history is likely to assert itself. What we've already had to handle with the others may seem like minor upsets by comparison."

Except it wouldn't likely be her who would face those crises. "You'll want to tell that to Helen."

His jaw worked. "If I hire her."

"You will. Estelle showed me her résumé." A throbbing

started in her chest at the reminder of how soon she'd be leaving. "I spoke with Phillip last night. He's got a job waiting for me in L.A."

Tension drew harsh lines on his face. "Is he waiting for you as well?"

"I don't want Phillip back in my life."

"I wonder what it is you do want."

She had no answer for him. When she didn't respond, he dropped his gaze to the papers on his desk. "Let me know if any issues come up with the new girls."

On Thursday morning, while she oversaw Ruby instructing Shawna and Maria in how to make pie dough, she kept one eye on the clock. Tony had scheduled Helen's interview at ten o'clock. At two minutes before the hour, Rebecca spotted the woman walking across the yard toward Tony's office. Helen looked to be in her forties, her hair short and no-nonsense, the slacks and short-sleeved blouse she wore plain and workmanlike.

She was still there when she and the teens took a break at ten-thirty. At eleven-thirty, when Rebecca left the house on her way back to the bakeshop, Helen's car was still parked in the lot. Rebecca was about to step inside the kitchen when she heard Tony call out to her from his office door.

"Can I have a minute?"

She guessed that he wanted her to talk to Helen, to give him her impression of the applicant. She should feel flattered that he valued her opinion. Instead, her heart just weighed even heavier in her chest.

After telling Ruby she was in charge for lunch prep, Rebecca headed toward Tony's office. As she walked the path, the late summer heat bathed her face with a pleasant warmth. She remembered this time of year—the loveliness of the days, the nights cool with hints of the autumn to come. As brutal as the summers could be in the Sacramento Valley, September and October provided a lovely respite between searing heat and winter storms.

In L.A., the seasons scarcely varied. Except in the San Fernando Valley, the temperatures cruised along at a temperate setting year-round. The trees didn't dress in orange and red and yellow in the fall, there were no hillsides rippling with vivid green grass in the spring. When she first moved to Southern California, she'd loved the sameness. But this short visit back home reminded her how much she'd missed the spectacular play of color in the Sacramento Valley when autumn painted the liquidambar trees with shimmering gold.

Tony waited for her at the door, stepping aside to let her pass. Helen sat in the same chair Rebecca had when she'd interviewed back in July. The older woman rose, putting her hand out for Rebecca to shake.

Helen's broad smile transformed the plainness of her face. "Considering all the stellar reports I've heard about you from Tony, I can't understand why he's interviewing me to take your place."

Rebecca glanced over at him, could see nothing in the cool neutrality of his expression. "As much as I've enjoyed working here, I'm relocating back to L.A."

If Helen saw any of Rebecca's turmoil in her face, she was polite enough to ignore it. Tony invited Rebecca to sit in his chair. "I'm going up to the house to contact Helen's references."

He walked out, leaving Rebecca and Helen to chat in private. Tony had left Helen's résumé out on his desk.

Using it as a starting point, Rebecca quizzed Helen about her previous work experience as a high-school home-economics teacher and the mentor program she'd set up for foster children.

Helen answered each query with direct candor, keeping her gray gaze steady on Rebecca, her ready smile lighting her face every time she discussed the children she'd worked with. She related a long list of success stories, teens she'd helped through major crises. She also frankly shared a few less-than-happy endings, students whose failures she took personally and obviously still grieved over.

She shook her head, her smile sad. "It's hard to forget them, isn't it?"

Rebecca reflected for a moment, the faces of the eight teens swimming in her mind's eye. James's mischievous grin, Kevin's serious gaze. Ruby's intelligence, Katy's lightheartedness. Brittany's goofy sense of humor, Colleen's sweetness. The inseparable Serena and Ari, their sometimes sharp-edged tongues that would nevertheless soften when they spoke to Lea or Estelle.

Lea and Estelle—how would she leave them behind? Doubts buffeted her as her heart knotted even tighter.

Thankfully, Tony knocked just then and stepped inside. From behind Helen, he lifted a brow, silently asking Rebecca for her feedback. She nodded, giving Tony a thumbs-up.

He crossed to the desk. "Everyone had great things to say about you, Helen. When can you start?"

The older woman's smile increased its wattage. As she and Tony consulted a calendar to look at dates, Rebecca slipped out the door. She'd find out when her last day would be soon enough.

Turning from the path, she crossed the lawn to the house, letting herself inside. She held herself together until she shut the door of her room, then sank to the edge of her narrow twin bed. Tears burned her eyes, clawed at her throat, but she forced herself to hold them back.

There'd be plenty of time to cry on the long trip back to L.A.

After spending the next weekend observing, Helen started working with the teens the following Monday. As Tony expected, the group eyed her with suspicion, unwilling to trust anyone new. Change had been a constant in their lives, and it had rarely augured anything good. They intended to make Helen work for their respect.

But from the outset, Tony could see his choice had been a good one. She had a different approach than Rebecca, more no-nonsense than empathetic, a little more authoritarian. Still loving, still caring, but Helen made it clear from the outset that she would be their boss and not their friend.

As Rebecca stepped back more and more during Helen's two-week trial, the dynamic shifted. Rebecca's more frenetic style gave way to Helen's rigid discipline. At first the teens bridled against the older woman's tighter control. But for the most part, they'd all changed in the month and a half they'd been with the program, had matured even in those short six weeks. They were ready for Helen. Even Shawna and Maria, in desperate need of structure, took well to her.

As the days of Helen's trial wore on, Tony barely kept his sanity. With Rebecca still living in his house, so close to him yet a million miles away, he struggled to survive each day. Sometimes she'd look at him when they crossed paths, she on her way to the bakeshop, he on his way to his office, and the profound sorrow in her eyes all but wrenched his heart from his chest.

The next weekend Helen supervised the teens as they ran the bakeshop. Deep down inside, Tony had almost hoped she'd prove incompetent, would fall apart under pressure. But from her skill in the kitchen to her compassion when Shawna had a meltdown, it was clear she was a keeper.

Monday morning, he sought out Estelle in the bunkhouse. After two and a half weeks on her new medication, his former foster mom looked better than she had in quite a while. At least he didn't have worry over Estelle to add to the rest of the wrangle inside him.

Estelle sat reading the *Sacramento Bee* on one of the sofas. Brittany and Lea were sprawled out on the floor, sharing a box of crayons and a coloring book.

"Brittany, would you take Lea over to the house?" Tony asked. "Bring back that book on the coffee table in the living room. It's for Grams." He hadn't finished the novel, but it gave him an excuse to send Lea away.

After they'd gone, Tony sat beside Estelle. "What do you think of Helen?"

Estelle folded the newspaper and set it aside. "She's great. A good complement for Becca."

"She's replacing Rebecca."

"But does she have to?"

"Rebecca said she's leaving, Estelle. I didn't ask her to. It was her choice."

Estelle linked her hands in her lap. "But you don't want her to go."

Frustration welled up inside him. "What am I supposed to do? Beg her not to?"

"You know she loves you."

"She loved me before. That didn't keep her with me."

"Do you love her?" Estelle asked quietly.

"Yes." There was no way he couldn't speak the truth to her. "As much as I ever did."

"Then why—"

"Because she's leaving," he said savagely. "I could tell her I love her. That I don't care how long she stays. That I'd take whatever time she's willing to give me."

Feeling ready to explode, he pushed to his feet. "But how can I put Lea on that razor's edge? Put her through that torment, never knowing when Rebecca might change her mind? I can't. Lea comes first. I don't give a damn how it makes me feel."

"How do you know she wouldn't stay if you asked her to?"

"It can't be because I ask her." He sank back down beside Estelle. "She has to get there on her own."

With a sigh, he shut his eyes, his head falling against the sofa back. "Tonight, I'm going to tell Helen she's got the job."

"Then I should move into the house. Let Helen have my room." Sam had put Helen up in a local motel for the short term.

He sat up, scrubbed at his face. "Yeah. It would be awkward to have her share the house with me. Especially once Rebecca leaves."

She patted his cheek, the way she'd done when he'd had a rotten day at school as a kid. "It'll all work out, Antonio."

He had to hope it would. He gave her a hug and got to

his feet. On his way back to his office, he saw Brittany and Lea returning from the house.

He waited for them on the path. Lea ran toward him, her eyes bright with love for him. When she reached him, he picked her up and held her close.

"Daddy, can I tell you a secret?" she whispered in his ear.

"Sure, *mija.*"

Her small arms wrapped around his neck. "I don't want Becca to leave. I wish we could make her stay. I'll be scared without her."

He gulped in a breath as emotion overwhelmed him. He realized Lea was crying. Before he could even think about how to comfort her, she wriggled from his grasp and hit the ground running. Brittany hurried after her, leaving him alone on the path.

By eight o'clock Thursday morning, Rebecca's bags were packed. She'd printed out detailed notes for Helen about every aspect of the program that she'd developed in the nearly two months she'd been there. She had only to say her last goodbyes to the teens, already on their way to the bakeshop. She'd heard Tony leave a half hour ago, no doubt for his office.

Last night's farewell party had been bittersweet, the teens standing up one by one to thank her, to describe what they'd learned from her, whether it was how to make the perfect white sauce or how to keep your cool when you're under the gun. Then Serena and Ari brought out a cake they'd made and decorated in secret, *Goodbye, Rebecca* inscribed across it. Rebecca had burst into tears, and the teens had enveloped her in a mass hug.

She took a last scan of her room, then checked the bathroom for anything left behind. Only Estelle's odds and ends remained crowded on the left side of the counter. The right side where she'd arranged her own toiletries was empty. In the bedroom, her bed was stripped.

She sat on the edge of the bare mattress, loathe to take her final steps from the room. The last few days of sharing this space with Estelle had been like a doorway to the past. She couldn't talk about the present, couldn't bring herself to discuss what was going on between her and Tony. But the old memories seemed like safe ground.

So they reminisced about the time she'd spent at Estelle's. There were the Valentine's cards her foster mother helped her make for her parents and for Tony. The Easter basket Estelle hid for her and Tony to find. The Mother's Day visit to the rehabilitation hospital where her parents lived for that long year.

Fourth of July fireworks and summer picnics, the Halloween trick-or-treating with Tony. Thanksgiving crowded around the table with other fosters, present and past, Tony, Sam and Darius as close as any brothers could be. Christmas with a surprise visit from her parents, shortly before they were finally released to return home.

Rebecca realized she would have to find a way to keep Estelle in her life. She would arrange to fly her former foster mother down to Los Angeles, have her stay with her. She had sublet her condo in West L.A. in expectation of giving it up when the lease came due. Now that she would be moving back in, she'd have a spare room for Estelle.

Vanessa's room. The place she'd prepared for the daughter she'd hoped for, but could never have. Lea wouldn't be her daughter, either. She didn't have the heart to again consider adopting.

Closing the door on her dark thoughts, she hefted her two large suitcases and toted them out of the bedroom. As she expected, no sign of Tony. If he wasn't in the bakeshop with the others, she'd have to go over to his office to say her farewells.

But when she carried the suitcases outside, she didn't see Tony's Suburban in the parking lot. As she walked out to her car, she looked around her, thinking he might have moved it elsewhere on the ranch. But the truck was gone. Tony was gone.

She'd told him she'd be heading out between eight and nine. Yet he'd left without saying goodbye.

She swallowed back the pain as she stowed her suitcases in the trunk. Returning to the house, she hooked the bag of gifts from the teens over her arm, then grabbed her purse and toiletries. She knew from Estelle the teens had shopped at the thrift store in Placerville, but all of them, even the two new girls, had lovingly chosen something for her.

Everything packed away, she went to the bakeshop. The ten teens were waiting for her, and Estelle had brought Lea over. One after another, they gave her tearful hugs, begged her to come back for a visit.

Lea was the hardest. The little girl clung so tightly to Rebecca's neck she thought Lea would never let go.

Rebecca pressed a kiss to the top of Lea's head. "I love you, sweetheart."

"Me, too." Lea took in a shuddering breath. "There was a wishing star last night. I made a wish."

Lea relaxed her hold then and gave Rebecca a peck on the cheek. Rebecca let her go, then gave Estelle a last hug.

"Do you know where Tony went?" she asked the older woman.

"No idea," Estelle said.

Despair washed over her. Waving one last time, she walked away, out of the bakeshop and across the yard to her car. About to start the engine, she realized she'd forgotten the water bottle she'd filled and left in the refrigerator.

She considered leaving it, picking up water in town. But it had been one of her gifts, a plastic water bottle with a silly cartoon cat from Katy. If Katy found out she hadn't taken it with her, she'd be crushed.

Now she wanted nothing more than to be on her way. Hurrying inside the house, she crossed to the kitchen and found the chilled water bottle. When she turned to leave again, she spotted the package wrapped in brown paper on the kitchen table.

Her name was written across it in Tony's scrawl. She almost dropped the water as she set it aside. Her hands shook as she lifted the package, its size and shape familiar.

Ripping off the paper, a sob caught in her throat. Her own face smiled up at her, Tony with his cocky grin standing beside her in the photo. Her wearing the off-white cocktail dress she'd scoured the thrift store for, him in the suit borrowed from Jake. Love and hope shining in their eyes.

Clasping the photo to her chest, she swept up the water bottle and ran to the car. The framed wedding picture on the seat beside her, she pulled from the parking lot and onto the road. Her mind whirled a thousand miles an hour as she made her way to Highway 50.

In a moment of brilliant insight, she knew where he was. Maybe he left because he didn't want a goodbye—or he couldn't bear one. The message he intended the wedding photo to convey might have been good riddance—or please, don't forget me. It didn't matter. She was going after him.

The drive down Highway 50 seemed endless. He'd left close to an hour ago—he might not even still be there. She might pass him on the freeway.

But when she pulled through the cemetery gates, then along the winding road to Alejandro's gravesite, Tony's Suburban was still there.

Now that she was here, she tried to order her scrambled thoughts to figure out what she would say to him. But then she realized it didn't matter what she was thinking. It was what was in her heart that mattered.

He was kneeling in the grass, his back to her as she approached. He turned, pushing to his feet.

He stood there, motionless, staring down at her as she stood toe to toe with him. She tried to read his face, to parse out his mind, his heart. She tipped precariously between joy and desolation.

Then he threw his arms around her, pulling her so tightly against his chest she could barely breathe. Except she didn't care, would have given up breathing if it meant he would always be with her.

His mouth moved against her ear. "I would have come after you. I was going to let you get to L.A., realize how much you missed me. Missed Lea."

"It didn't take that long." She pressed against him, so grateful to have found him again. "I just couldn't leave."

He leaned back, his gaze so full of love he didn't have to speak the words aloud. Yet when he said "I love you, Becca," the sounds filled her heart to bursting.

"I love you, Tony." She raised on tiptoe to kiss him.

"Before, I couldn't stay. This time, I couldn't leave. I'm yours as long as you want me."

"How does forever sound?"

He drew her close again, holding her against his heart. In that peaceful place where they'd lain their son to rest, Rebecca pictured Alejandro watching them, a smile on his baby face. Joyous that his parents were together again at last.

Epilogue

"Serena, Ari!" Helen called out. "Stop your gossiping and sit. The wedding's about to start."

Standing in his living room beside the justice of the peace, Tony tugged at the collar of his tux shirt and wished he could strip off his bow tie. The jitters that had bubbled up the moment he took his place here made no sense. He'd been looking forward to this mid-December wedding for three months now. After he'd failed to convince Rebecca of the merits of a quickie Tahoe ceremony, he'd been eagerly counting the days until they could tie the knot.

Serena and Ari finally took their seats beside the other teens. To make room for the twenty or so folding chairs, Kevin and James had cleared out the furniture yesterday, toting it all into the newly built modular that would soon be Estelle and Helen's home. With Ruby hired on as Tony's new assistant and housemother for Estelle's House, she'd be in charge of keeping tabs on the next group of students. Rebecca and Helen would be sharing kitchen duties, allowing the program to increase class size.

On Tony's other side, Sam slapped him on the back. "No second thoughts?"

"Only that I wish we'd eloped."

Darius sat in the front row with Estelle, a space between them for Lea when she finished her flower-girl duties. His daughter was upstairs with the bride and Ruby, who was Rebecca's maid of honor.

"Still no word from Jana?" Sam asked.

Tony shook his head. "Cell phone's disconnected. No listing for her in Portland."

The wedding march started up then, and Tony's gaze whipped toward the stairs. He lasered in on the door to his bedroom.

Lea emerged first, dressed in a lemon-yellow dress full of frills and bows. Her dark hair was upswept, her face serious as she carried her basket to the stairs. She reached into her basket and solemnly dropped petals, one at a time, as she descended.

Ruby, in the doorway now, whispered loudly, "More, sweetpea. More petals."

By then Lea was nearly to the bottom. Gripping the side of the basket, she flung the contents into the air, petals flying everywhere. Everyone laughed, and Lea grinned as she ran the rest of the way to her seat between Darius and Estelle.

Ruby had already started down the stairs with her bouquet of white daisies and yellow roses, her knee-length yellow dress a nice contrast to her dark skin. She'd been thrilled when Rebecca had chosen her as maid of honor over the other girls. Tony knew Rebecca saw a bit of herself in Ruby's intelligence and determination.

The volume of the music increased, signaling Rebecca's entrance. He swallowed against a dry throat as she stepped out onto the landing.

For a moment he couldn't breathe. Lost track of the music and the murmur of voices, the people crowding his living room, even Sam and the justice of the peace beside him. He saw only Rebecca, starting down the stairs in the same dress she'd worn to their wedding almost thirteen years ago.

When she took her place beside him, a vision in cream colored lace and veil, he whispered, "How...?"

"Sam," Rebecca whispered back. "He had it duplicated from the old wedding photo."

Tony glanced over and saw the smug look on his friend's face. Then, as the justice of the peace recited the familiar opening to the wedding ceremony, he took Rebecca's hand, ready to face the rest of his life with his beloved.

* * * * *

CELEBRATE
60 YEARS
OF PURE READING PLEASURE
WITH HARLEQUIN®!

We'll be spotlighting a different series
every month throughout 2009
to celebrate our 60th anniversary.

Look for Harlequin® Blaze™ in March!

O-6O

*After all, a lot can happen in 60 years,
or 60 minutes...or 60 seconds!*

Find out what's going down in Blaze's
heart-stopping new miniseries *0-60!*
Getting from "Hello" to "How was it?"
can happen fast....

Look for the brand-new 0-60 miniseries in March 2009!

www.eHarlequin.com   HBRIDE09

HARLEQUIN® *Romance*®

This February the Harlequin® Romance series will feature six Diamond Brides stories featuring diamond proposals and gorgeous grooms.

Share your dream wedding proposal and you could WIN!

The most romantic entry will win a diamond necklace and will inspire a proposal in one of our upcoming Diamond Grooms books in 2010.

In 100 words or less, tell us the most romantic way that you dream of being proposed to.

For more information, and to enter the Diamond Brides Proposal contest, please visit **www.DiamondBridesProposal.com**

Or mail your entry to us at:

IN THE U.S.: 3010 Walden Ave., P.O. Box 9069, Buffalo, NY 14269-9069
IN CANADA: 225 Duncan Mill Road, Don Mills, ON M3B 3K9

www.eHarlequin.com   HRCONTESTFEB09

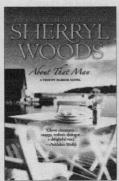 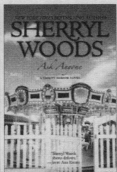 

REQUEST YOUR FREE BOOKS!

2 FREE NOVELS PLUS 2 FREE GIFTS!

SPECIAL EDITION®

Life, Love and Family!

YES! Please send me 2 FREE Silhouette Special Edition® novels and my 2 FREE gifts (gifts are worth about $10). After receiving them, if I don't wish to receive any more books, I can return the shipping statement marked "cancel." If I don't cancel, I will receive 6 brand-new novels every month and be billed just $4.24 per book in the U.S. or $4.99 per book in Canada, plus 25¢ shipping and handling per book and applicable taxes, if any*. That's a savings of at least 15% off the cover price! I understand that accepting the 2 free books and gifts places me under no obligation to buy anything. I can always return a shipment and cancel at any time. Even if I never buy another book from Silhouette, the two free books and gifts are mine to keep forever.

235 SDN EEYU   335 SDN EEY6

Name	(PLEASE PRINT)
Address	Apt. #
City	State/Prov. Zip/Postal Code

Signature (if under 18, a parent or guardian must sign)

Mail to the Silhouette Reader Service:
IN U.S.A.: P.O. Box 1867, Buffalo, NY 14240-1867
IN CANADA: P.O. Box 609, Fort Erie, Ontario L2A 5X3

Not valid to current subscribers of Silhouette Special Edition books.

Want to try two free books from another line?
Call 1-800-873-8635 or visit www.morefreebooks.com.

* Terms and prices subject to change without notice. N.Y. residents add applicable sales tax. Canadian residents will be charged applicable provincial taxes and GST. Offer not valid in Quebec. This offer is limited to one order per household. All orders subject to approval. Credit or debit balances in a customer's account(s) may be offset by any other outstanding balance owed by or to the customer. Please allow 4 to 6 weeks for delivery. Offer available while quantities last.

Your Privacy: Silhouette is committed to protecting your privacy. Our Privacy Policy is available online at www.eHarlequin.com or upon request from the Reader Service. From time to time we make our lists of customers available to reputable third parties who may have a product or service of interest to you. If you would prefer we not share your name and address, please check here. ☐

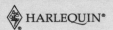

HARLEQUIN®

INTRIGUE®

SPECIAL OPS

TEXAS

COWBOY COMMANDO

BY JOANNA WAYNE

When Linney Kingston's best friend dies in
a drowning accident one day after she told
Linney she was leaving her abusive husband,
Linney is convinced the husband killed her. Linney
goes to the one man she knows can help her, an
ex lover who she's never been able to forget—
Navy SEAL Cutter Martin. They will have to
work together to solve the mystery, but can
they leave their past behind them?

Available March 2009 wherever you buy books.

The Inside Romance newsletter has a NEW look for the new year!

Same great content, brand-new look!

The Inside Romance newsletter is a FREE quarterly newsletter highlighting our upcoming series releases and promotions!

Click on the Inside Romance link on the front page of **www.eHarlequin.com** or e-mail us at insideromance@harlequin.ca to sign up to receive your FREE newsletter today!

You can also subscribe by writing to us at: HARLEQUIN BOOKS Attention: Customer Service Department P.O. Box 9057, Buffalo, NY 14269-9057

Please allow 4-6 weeks for delivery of the first issue by mail.

You're invited to join our Tell Harlequin Reader Panel!

By joining our new reader panel you will:

- Receive Harlequin® books—they are FREE and yours to keep with no obligation to purchase anything!
- Participate in fun online surveys
- Exchange opinions and ideas with women just like you
- Have a say in our new book ideas and help us publish the best in women's fiction

In addition, you will have a chance to win great prizes and receive special gifts!
See Web site for details. Some conditions apply.
Space is limited.

To join, visit us at
www.TellHarlequin.com.

COMING NEXT MONTH
Available February 24, 2009